THE EMANCIPATION OF DEBORAH

JAMES

By Dijon M McIntyre

PROLOGUE

There's a reason they call it Alabama The Beautiful. It's lush green mountains, crop filled fields, and simple country life are all assets to its confounding beauty. Alabama is a place where I go when I want to escape or at least find somewhere that I can completely be myself. Somewhere where I can fly as free as the American eagle that soars across the sky in my backyard, where I can lie down in the freshly cut grass in the middle of the blazing southern summer heat. But even in saying all of these wonderful things about Alabama, I cannot forget the reality that I experienced there. A reality that did not always include a place where I could see the beautiful lush fields, or the beautiful green mountains. No, Alabama for me, was a place where I walked through an Egyptian-like wilderness, where I faced constant adversity in pursuit of a better life. It was a place where I felt like I was suffering, a place that I never thought I'd be free of. The truth is, I only use those positive adjectives to describe Alabama because I'm trying to preserve what little beauty I actually experienced there. In my mind, in the depths of my mind, that place was only one of darkness for me. An inescapable darkness that I longed to be free of. Now I'm about to invite you into that darkness, into the corners of my mind before they are taken over by the brain deteriorating disease—

Alzheimer's. I have to take you there so that

someone knows, because if I don't tell

anyone now, there may never be a chance to.

If I don't tell anyone about the truth that I've

been running from my entire life, then I will

never get a chance to experience *my*

freedom, *my* emancipation.

CHAPTER ONE

December 1st, 1933. That's the day I was born, the day that I was destined for a life of affliction. My momma, Pearly May Henderson, was nineteen years old when she gave birth to me. I was the second out of five children. There's my stern older sister, Snippy Henderson, my sweet younger brother, Jiren Henderson came after me. Then there's Eve Henderson "the wise one", and the baby, Samuel Henderson. My momma named me "Deborah Henderson", after Deborah in The Bible since momma was a very religious woman. Growing up, my momma always told me that she knew I was meant to become something from the day I was born. She claims I always gave her a lot of trouble but she fixed that real quick. There wasn't a thing I could get away with. She would always send one of my siblings, usually Snippy (since she was the eldest), outside and cut a switch off the tree. "And it better be a good one" momma would say, "cause if it ain't, I'm gonna beat her ass and yours too". Snippy would come back in with a switch so thick, you'd think it was a whole tree branch. Momma would tell me to go strip naked, and she would take the switches and soak them in hot water. I'd strip bare bones, and after about thirty minutes of quivering so hard with fear you would think I was about to go into a convulsive seizure, momma would take the switches out the water and the beating would begin. Whip! I heard it coming at me as if it was a quick rush of wind from outside. I'd scream in agonizing pain. Momma would tell me to shut up, then again, whip! And I'd scream again; Momma would tell me again to shut up. The process continued for what felt like hours but was only about ten minutes or so. She'd finally stop whenever the switch would break and she was out of switches to use. I'd be crying like a newborn baby, even when I was twelve or thirteen years old. It left some deep bruises on me, I ain't talking about the ones you get from chasing cute boys around the schoolyard and busting the flesh of your knees in the grass. I'm talking about bruises that were deep beneath the skin, that were multiple colors, from light red to a deep royal purple. Covering your whole body, from your face all the way down to your legs. Sometimes the pain from the bruises was so bad that I couldn't even sit down because my ass was too bruised up. But Momma always said that she only beat you if she loved you, that God only disciplines His children that He really cares about. I don't know if that was true but if it was then my momma darn near worshipped the ground I walked on cause she never hesitated to give me a good 'ole whooping. The thing that momma never understood is those beatings didn't just leave physical scars, they left mental and emotional ones too that would follow me my whole life. Her beatings in combination with a few other events in my life are exactly why I'm writing this story now. Don't get me wrong, I don't hate my momma at all. I just wish she chastised me in a way that I wouldn't have to suffer for decades later. 'Til this day I still remember every beating I got, but 'til this day I still love my Momma and I wish to God that she was still alive. Guess I should be careful what I wish for though, if she heard me using some of the language

I'm using then she'd give me another good 'ole beaten, even at 84 years old.

Besides getting the living daylights beat out of me, life in my house wasn't too bad. I always got along with my dad; he loved me to pieces. He would always call me his "special little girl" and treated me like it too. He would take me on long drives out to the farms to go pick up some fresh meat, milk, and vegetables for the family. It would be just me and him, riding through the beautiful state on a sunny Saturday morning, leaving the house at five and not coming back until four in the evening.

"Daddy, why do we always drive out to farms to get food? We can't just go to the meat market?" I would ask

"We could Deborah, but I prefer some time away from the house. I love looking at the different farmers and their crops and having a variety to choose from. Plus, I love being with you my special little princess," he would say with a big smile.

When we got to the house, we would wash up, prepare supper for the family, and eat until our heart's content. Daddy was such a good man, I always told myself that if I ever got married then I would marry someone who was just like him. He and I just had that special father-daughter bond that not everyone is blessed enough to have the opportunity to get. There's more than a few times that I remember daddy fixing issues going on in the house, both big and small. With he and momma having to raise five kids, there were plenty of times when daddy had to fix the toilet cause it was stopped up from excessive use, or he would forgo buying nice clothes for himself to make sure that we all looked elegant when we went to school. It never mattered about how much money we actually had, daddy made sure we looked like we came from a wealthy household every single time we walked out that door.

But all of that changed when I was twelve years old. I remember the day like it was yesterday. My siblings and I had just gotten home from school. We walked in the house and momma was cleaning up like always. We had put our things down and offered to help her, but for some reason, she didn't want any help. That alone was a bit unusual for her. Instead of asking me to help her, she sent me to go out to the garden to tend to the plants and water the vegetables. That was oftentimes my favorite thing to do because it required me being away from everyone else and having time to myself, which was valuable and rare in a big family like ours. As I was watering my mom's

favorite vegetable, her habanero peppers,
one of dad's best friends, who we called
"Papa Joe," came sprinting up to me,
panting like a dog in heat. I looked at him
and said,

"Papa Joe, everything alright?" He
began pouring out his tears and said to me,

"Debbie, you gotta come over to my
place, quick. It's an emergency." Without
asking much, I followed him over to his
place and there I saw him, my six foot tall
father laid out on the grass. Not moving. Not
breathing. A lifeless corpse. I asked Papa
Joe how long had he been lying there as I
was hoping this was just some kind of
temporary fainting issue, but the look on his

face and the constant flow of tears told me everything I needed to know, my daddy had gone to be with The Lord. Daddy was working outside in the blistering summer heat and had a stroke.

I took a deep breath and tried not to cry. 'Til this day I could not tell you how I was able to maintain such a calm composure but I'll chalk it up to being a master at hiding how I truly felt about the world around me. I looked at Papa Joe, who just stood there, weeping over my dad's dead body and told him that he needed to run down to the hospital and let them know what happened. Back in those days we didn't have the convenience of dialing 9-1-1. As he made his way up the road to the hospital, I stood over my dad's lifeless body and all I could do was stare at him. The man I loved more than anyone else in the world was now gone; I didn't know what to do. I figured that at some point I had to stop staring at what was no longer there and grab a hold of the reality that I was about to face. I said a prayer for my dad and I walked back over to my place. I knew I had to tell my mother about what had happened, but I had to figure out the right words to say to her. How do you tell a woman that the man she had been raising a family with, and who dedicated her life to was no longer alive, especially when that man was your father. But there was a reason that God had placed that yoke on my back. He would not have asked me to carry it if He didn't think I was capable of handling it. So, even with all my nervousness and grief, I walked inside my house and told my mother I needed to talk to her. She was initially dismissive towards me; this wasn't out of rudeness—she just was busy doing the housework. But I told her it was really important and my mother had never heard me say anything to her in a tone as serious as the one I used on that day. She stopped her work and looked at me almost as if she knew I was about to give her some news she didn't want to hear. I struggled to get the words out at first and then, out of frustration, I just told her,

"Daddy is gone, Momma, he's dead." After I said it, I could hardly believe that it was true myself, but the look on her face and the unfortunate timing of my siblings entering the room just as I told her confirmed the dark reality that we were faced with. She stared at me.

"What did you say?" I was afraid to repeat myself but knew if I didn't then she would "knock all the teeth out of my head," as she would say. I repeated it and she walked up to me and stared me down as if I was the devil and she had somehow become Christ in the form of a six foot tall woman.

Then much to the surprise of me and my on-looking siblings, she slapped me so hard that I fell down to the ground. My face was throbbing with pain and I gripped it with my hand for some sad attempt at comfort. I looked up at my mom and she pointed her index finger at me and said in the most terrifying whisper I've ever heard in my life, "You better not ever tell a lie like that again. You better be lucky that I don't make you strip down butt naked and beat you right now. Now get up and go outside and finish doing what I told you to do."

I couldn't believe it, I'd told my momma the truth and look at what I got in return. I didn't know what to do and neither did my siblings. They all just stared at the entire thing like it was some kind of live theatre performance.

After getting over the initial shock of just how hard my momma hit me, I got up and headed outside like I was told. I resumed doing the work I was assigned to do by my momma as if nothing at all had just happened. I kept replaying in my mind the conversation and the subsequent reaction by my momma. I still couldn't process it completely. My mind began racing as fast as a jack rabbit running towards a barrel of carrots. *What if my momma comes out here*

and beats me with a switch I asked myself. .
What do I say to her when I go back inside?
Is it even worth going back inside now that
daddy is gone? As these three questions
swirled around my mind, I happened to hear
fast footsteps coming up the driveway. I
turned my head just in time to see both the
doctor and Papa Joe approaching me. *Well* I
thought, *Momma may not accept my words*
but she won't refute what a doctor says.
They approached me, and Papa Joe looked
at me with a confused expression and said,

"Debbie, why aren't you inside
helpin' comfort your momma?" I replied,

"I tried to tell her what happened,
Papa Joe, but she ain't wanna listen."

He said, "What do you mean? You told her that your dad passed away didn't you?"

"Yeah," I told him. "I told her but she called me a liar and slapped me so hard that she knocked my teeth crooked."

"My God, she must be in shock. Now why don't you stay right here while Dr. Taylor here and I go explain to her what happened,"

"Papa Joe, if you don't mind, I'd like to come with you when you tell her. She is my momma after all."

"Alright Debbie, you can join us. Just make sure you stay close to me wouldn't want your momma taking her frustration out on a beautiful little girl such as yourself," he said as he smiled at me. So we went inside and initially momma was very kind and welcoming, almost as if I hadn't told her anything. I contributed to her being a southern woman and being raised to always be polite when you have guests in the house. But, the moment Papa Joe said he needed to have a talk with her and that it was serious, her expression began to change.

"What is it, Joe? She said. "Did something happen with my husband"?

"I don't know how to tell you this big momma but, he…he had a heart attack" he said. Momma didn't reply, she just looked at him straight in the eyes like she did me, I was afraid she was gonna attack him too. She then turned her gaze towards me and said,

"Now Debbie, I should beat your ass for not only telling Papa Joe about this fabricated story you came up with but for making him go get a doctor. Doctor I'm so sorry that my daughter wasted your precious time but give me a price and I'll pay you so you can be on your way." Doctor Taylor just looked at Papa Joe, who was trying to keep himself from crying. Papa Joe finally mustered up the courage to say,

"I'm sorry big momma, it's true. I'm the one who told Debbie about it. Ben had a heart attack while we were working in the yard and Dr. Taylor here confirmed that his spirit has departed to the other side."

Momma froze. The reality was slowly creeping up on her, I could see it in her face. She began welling up with tears, though she did her best to fight back, but her efforts just weren't enough. She walked back to her room and slammed the door so hard that the family picture on the wall in the living room plundered to the ground. Dr. Taylor and Papa Joe were left speechless, both with their hands on my shoulders, seemingly trying to comfort me. But I think they were the ones who needed the comfort, especially Papa Joe.

After a few seconds of dead silence coming from my momma's room, we heard a loud cry like the sound of a banshee. Then we heard what sounded like chairs and God knows what else being thrown around her bedroom and up against the walls. I was terrified. Seeing that as a little girl did something to me. Made me rethink what it meant to be a strong person. Up until that point I'd hardly ever seen momma show so much emotion so I knew that whatever she was feeling was the most powerful and uncontrollable emotion she had ever felt before. Papa Joe told Dr. Taylor to take me outside and that he was gonna get my siblings out the house too. He said we shouldn't see our momma like this and he was right, damn near made me have a heart attack—and that's the last thing that needed to happen.

After we were all taken outside, Papa Joe told us to follow him to his house. We stayed the night there, though there wasn't much room for us. I could hardly sleep that night thinking about daddy and what state momma was in. In fact, it bothered me so much that I got out of bed and somehow managed to sneak past all my siblings without waking any of them. I went to the kitchen and saw Papa Joe drinking some dark liquor straight out the bottle. He didn't notice me at first and I thought about just going back to my room and going to sleep, but as I began to turn around, he noticed me.

"Debbie? What are you doing up at this time of night?"

"I don't know" I told him. "I just couldn't sleep thinking about what happened to daddy." He looked at me for a minute and told me to come sit on the couch with him. This was a bit of a strange gesture I thought to myself but it was late, and he was drunk, so I figured I better not argue.

When we got to the sofa, he looked at me and asked me if I wanted a sip of his alcohol. I told him no, that I didn't think I was allowed to drink since I wasn't old enough. He said, "It'll make the pain better. Don't worry, I won't tell your momma or anyone else. It'll be our little secret." I hesitated but there was something about his calming nature and attractive smile that made me give in to his offer. I took a big sip and it burned me so bad that tears began welling in my eyes. Papa Joe laughed, not mockingly though, more so in the way of a father watching their child do something new and failing at it. He then wiped the tears from my eyes and looked at me in the eyes and said to me, "Debbie, I want you to know that you were your father's favorite child. He loved you more than anyone else in the world, he would have given anything in order to make you happy. I just want to know that."

"Thank you, Papa Joe," I said. "I'm gonna head to bed now."

"Debbie wait."

"If you're gonna offer me more to drink, I think I'll pass," I told him.

"No, I need you to put your hands right here." He pointed to his groin area.

"Papa Joe, I'm old enough to know what that is. Why are you asking me to touch you there," I asked him. I couldn't for the life in me believe that Papa Joe was asking me to touch him there. All I could think is *why is he asking me to do this?*

Doesn't he know that I'm a child? Is he just trying to take advantage of the fact that my dad is gone now? His next words got me out of my head and into the strange reality that I was in the middle of.

"If you're old enough to know what it is, then you already know why I'm asking you," he replied. We stared at each other for a minute as my heart began to race with an unspeakable anxiety and fear that can't be put into words. I swallowed heavily and walked towards him, slowly unzipped his pants and did as he asked. "That a girl Debbie, just keep touching just like that." We kept going until he finished.

After that he kissed me on my forehead and told me to go to bed. I couldn't sleep that night at all, I had just done something that was foreign to my twelve year old mind, and I didn't know how to feel honestly. The worst part is I'd like to tell you that was the only time that happened to me, but that night was only one of many that would shape the rest of my life.

CHAPTER TWO

About two or three years after the
death of father, I went out to get a job to
help provide for the family. With my dad no
longer around to help with bills and such,
things begin to get really stressful for
momma. Now of course she had help from
some of family members and from Papa Joe
but, I couldn't stand to see my momma
struggle anymore. My siblings could have
gotten a job but truthfully they were more
focused on their education and I was more
on providing for the family. That's what dad
always taught me, that no matter what I
should be willing to give all of myself to

help those in need. So I took heed and went and made one of the biggest decisions of my life: I decided to drop out of school. When I had first told momma about it, she wasn't too fond of my decision, but when I explained that I just wanted to help, she relented. Now this was a bit unusual for momma to do as she had pride on being an independent woman, even when daddy was alive, but she knew the reality of the situation she faced was enough to make her put her pride to the side. I drove out to the farm area where daddy and I always used to go to get fresh fruits and vegetables for the house. I thought to myself that even though my skills were limited, there were a few things I knew how to do exceptionally well due to the way momma raised me: cook, clean, and take care of people. In those days I didn't have no resume like I would have to have today to work even a starter job like McDonald's this worked to my advantage. I drove up to various farmers' ranches and told them I was looking for work. They would oftentimes look at me and wonder what exactly it was I needed a job for at my age. Many of them accused me of having a baby out of wedlock and assumed that's why. But I explained the situation about my daddy being gone, and being that some of them remember me with him, they were sympathetic towards me. Now unfortunately, that sympathy didn't mean that they were willing or able to hire me on, but they did donate money and food to me which I greatly appreciated.

It was nearing sundown when I finally managed to get somewhere. His name was Mr. Ben and he owned a huge piece of land with every kind of animal and plant you could think of. I had never been to his farm with my father, only we had passed by it a few times when we would take a side road and just spend time talking and laughing with each other. I missed those days more than anything, but I couldn't hold on to what was no longer there. I went up to

Mr. Ben's door, knocked, and introduced myself. He did the same and flashed a smile at me (that I must admit made me blush on the account of his attractiveness as an older white man.) He invited me in when I explained to him what I was there for and offered me something to eat. I tried to reject it but he was quite insistent, and because of some of the rules of southern hospitality, I knew it would be rude of me to keep saying no. We talked and got to know each other and established a good friendship within a few minutes of me being there.

"So tell me Deborah, what brings a young girl like you around here?"

"Well as I mentioned earlier, I was looking for some work to help provide for my family. My daddy recently passed away and my momma can't do it all on her own even though she tries to"

"I see, I'm sorry to hear that Deborah." He grabbed my hand and tried to comfort me. I was a little hesitant since I didn't know him that well but something about him made me feel like I could trust him.

I spilled my heart to Mr. Ben and looking back on it, I know why. He had a familiar feel about him that reminded me of Papa Joe, at least the good parts of him that I experienced when I went over his house with my father. Perhaps the fact that he was an older white man might have played a part in this familiarity, but it wasn't the main reason. It was the way he talked, how he held my hand and comforted me as I talked about the pain I felt from losing my father. In all honesty we had become so sidetracked talking about my dad that I forgot my original purpose in going to see him.

After an hour or so of talking and giving him my life story, we finally got to why I was there. I told him I wanted to get a job to help out my momma and he was surprisingly impressed and very empathetic. He told me that his wife spends a lot of time going out of town with their kids and that he doesn't usually get the chance to join them since he works a lot. He explained that he had little time to cook, clean, or care for the farm. I didn't say anything to him but that certainly helped to explain why his food looked—and smelled— questionable. He agreed to hire me for twenty-five cents an hour. Now that may sound a bit comical to anyone nowadays, but back then it was considered to be well above the minimum wage. When he made the offer to me I almost fainted, I couldn't believe that someone like me would be making that much money at my age, and with me being a woman. But who was I to doubt the blessings of God, all I knew was that this could be the ultimate thing to not only help my mother out, but to free our whole household from the pains of debt and lack. This money would be our true emancipation. After accepting his offer and thanking him with a warm yet impulsive hug, I got my things and prepared to leave. Before I walked out, Mr. Ben stopped me and looked me in the eyes for a few seconds, and I started to become nervous. Not in a bad way, but in the way a person does before they do something that they've been anticipating. I asked him why was he staring at me and he told me I was one of the most beautiful people that he'd ever seen, that I reminded him of one of those negros who would go down in history for doing something big. I didn't know what to think of this or how to react to it and my face must have given that message because he immediately felt the need to explain himself and apologize. I stopped him and told him that it wasn't necessary and that I completely understood what he was saying to me, although truthfully I didn't at all. He then pulled me in for a hug and said he couldn't wait to see me tomorrow at 3:00 P.M. sharp. I blessed him and went on my way.

When I arrived home it was well into the night and my momma was up waiting for me. I was afraid that she was getting ready to give me a beating so I started explaining myself as fast I could, despite fumbling over my words. She told me to calm down and that she wasn't going to do anything to me. She was just happy to know that I was home safely. I explained what happened with Mr. Ben and the very gracious offer that he made me. Momma almost fainted as well from being so shocked, but once she got herself together she expressed her joy and support for what I was doing. She started singing old spirituals to the Lord and tried to get me to join in. Even though I didn't join in on her singing, I cannot tell you how good it made me feel to know that I was now doing something that really made my momma proud of me. That's all I wanted ever since my dad died, to make my momma proud and give her at least some of the love she felt when my daddy was here.

CHAPTER THREE

I was getting ready for my first day at work with Mr. Ben. I put on the best clothes that I had and said a prayer before I left the house. I asked the Lord to let His will be done and to work through me for what I was about to do. As I was driving there, visions kept flashing across my mind about what it would be like working for a white man. See, now I didn't have anything against white people in the least bit, but there were a lot of racial tensions going on between white people and negros in those days. I was only the second generation out of slavery, so needless to say, I had some reservations. Of course I grew up with a white neighbor, Papa Joe, who up until a few years ago had never done anything out of the ordinary to me. Even when he did do a few things that were questionable, it never made me think of him as a racist man.

As I entered Mr. Ben's house, I was lead to a table of uncooked food. He looked at me and said,

"You know how to cook, right?"

"Of course" I told him. "In my household, I was always eager to learn how to cook from the soul." A big grin spread across his face that showed his pearly white teeth and somehow made his baby blue eyes pop for the first time.

"Well, here I have freshly de-feathered chicken, three bunches of collard greens, a handful of habanero peppers, freshly picked bell peppers, a jug of milk straight from the cow, and every kind of seasoning you can imagine," he told me. I was speechless, here I had everything I could ever want to cook at my disposal, and yet this was something I was supposed to get paid for. Mr. Ben could see the shock written across my face, although he wasn't sure how to take it. He asked me if I was okay and if this was too much for me to handle. I looked at him and told him,

"Mr. Ben, this is nothing short of a biggest blessing I ever received from The Lord Jesus Christ Himself." He laughed and told me,

"I'll take that as your way of saying thank you, although I'm not sure what for. I explained to him that I was just honored to have a chance to serve him in this way and, furthermore, that I have a true passion for cooking. He understood and was impressed at my passion. "Well, cook 'til your heart's content. I have an important business meeting tonight and everyone is always more willing to listen when they're well fed."

"Okay. I will whip up something that'll make your taste buds holler," I promised him. "I have faith you will" he said as he smiled at me and walked away. Now I can't lie, I was about as intimidated as I could be. I wasn't just cooking for one white man who obviously had a lot of money; I was cooking for a *group* of white men who had a lot of money. I knew that if I messed up on this, it would be the absolute end of my job and momma would be devastated. All I could think of was daddy and what I could do to honor his name through whatever I cooked. So, I began to work immediately. First, I wiped down everything in the kitchen, from the sink to the inside of the refrigerator. I had to make sure there wasn't gonna be any kind of infection or sickness spread through the good work that The Lord was about to do through me in this meal. Once I was done cleaning and making sure everything was spotless, I began the prep. I washed the greens in a round tub at least three times to make sure there wasn't gone be any bugs or dirt left on them. While they were soaking, I began cleaning the chicken and cutting off the fat and excess skin. Then I chopped a few things up— onions, the bell peppers, just a few things to help the meal have a bit more flavor to it. I seasoned the chicken with Lawry's seasoning salt and let it marinate for a few hours. All of this was an exact replica of my very first meal I made on my own for daddy when I was about ten years old. Even though I knew I wasn't actually cooking for him, I worked as if I was.

While I was prepping, Mr. Ben walked by a few times and after about the third time I stopped him. I said to him in a light-hearted playful manner

"Now I hope you trust me, I'm not gonna do anything to this food that would harm you. That would be a disservice to both you and the good Lord."

"I apologize if I startled you, I was just interested in how much effort you put into your food. It's truly inspiring."

"Thank you Mr. Ben, I just work with all my heart." He gently smiled at me and walked away, I felt very encouraged after hearing him say my cooking was inspiring.

After I got everything in the process of being cooked, it clicked in me that something was missing. How on Earth would I feed all these rich white men coming in without giving them any kind of dessert? I went through the fridge and freezer to see what I could whip up that wouldn't be too high maintenance, since I had only about an hour to finish everything. After searching through the massive amounts of food he had, I noticed some peaches in the bottom of the fridge. I quickly grabbed them and the flour I had used for the fried chicken and started making some of my dad's favorite homemade peach cobbler. There weren't many things daddy would make but he always made it a goal to make peach cobbler on holidays, birthdays, any special occasion really. By the time I got that in the oven, the dinner finished cooking. Just in time too, 'cause the doorbell rang, and Mr. Ben called for me to answer it since he was in the shower. I went to the door and two plump white men stood right of me with a rather shocked face as if they had gone to the wrong house.

"Is Benjamin here?" one of them said.

"Yes sir, he is," I replied.

"Where is he?" the other one said in a deeper, almost antagonistic tone.

"He's getting dressed right now but you're welcome to come in and sit down." They both looked at each other, then walked in almost cautiously. As they came in and took a seat, the first one talked to me and formally introduced himself. "I'm William

Jones and this is my brother Evan Jones, we both work with Benjamin."

"It's a pleasure to formally meet you both; my name is Deborah Henderson. I work for Mr. Ben."

"Work? You mean you're his slave," Evan said.

"Evan, have some manners! Slavery ended a long time ago!" Mr. William told him.

"It's quite alright Mr. William, I am here to work for Mr. Ben as his servant. Now some might call that slavery but it was a choice on my behalf and I'm being well compensated for my service." At the time that I said that, it hadn't occurred to me that I was in a house full of white males and I was quite a ways away from home. My comment could have been taken the wrong way and caused me my life, but all I could do was think about how rude and outdated Mr. Evan's comment was.

"Well that's a good thing Debbie, you mind if I call you Debbie?" Mr. William asked.

"No sir, I don't mind at all. Call me whatever you like," I replied.

"How about nigger?" Mr. Evan remarked.

"Evan, that's enough. You are being so disrespectful to this kind, beautiful young lady." Mr. William said. He continued,

"Please ignore my brother, his mind isn't exactly on the same level as us more intelligent beings." I gave a small laugh and it must have set Mr. Evan off because he stood immediately and started pointing and screaming,

"You think that's funny you nigger? Don't you know I'll knock the black off your ass!" I was too much in shock to say anything. I had never had an experience like this with anyone—much less white people—before.

Mr. Ben must have been listening in because he walked in swiftly and with an angered look on his face. I was terrified when I saw him and thought that it would be the end of my employment. Then, he went to Mr. Evan and said to him, "Evan, is there a problem?" Mr. Evan replied,

"I was just trying to keep your little slave here disciplined, that's all." Mr. Ben's anger intensified.

"Deborah isn't a slave, she's my employee that I hired personally because of her intelligence and eagerness to work to help provide for her family. I will not allow you or anyone else who steps in my house to disrespect her, no matter how you feel about negros. If that's a problem with you, then you can see yourself out of this meeting before Mr. Joseph arrives." I couldn't believe his words. Mr. Ben hardly knew me and surely didn't know me well enough to defend me to another one of his own kind. I suspect that they hadn't seen that side of Mr. Ben before because both Mr. Evan and Mr. William became about pale as a couple of ghosts. Mr. Evan took a step back from Mr. Ben and said,

"Okay Ben, I apologize. I was obviously out of place when I talked to your...employee. Please, forgive my ignorance." Before Mr. Ben could say anything else, the smell of the cobbler began to fill the house and it made me abruptly rush to the kitchen to make sure it wasn't burning. Mr. Ben followed me into the kitchen and I could see Mr. Evan and Mr. William resume their seats. Mr. Ben asked me, almost in a whisper,

"Are you okay Debbie?"

"Yes, Sir" I told him.

"I don't want you to be nervous," he continued. "These men do not own this house nor do you work for them, you work for me. Understand?"

"Yes, Sir" I told him. "I don't mean to be rude, Mr. Ben but I really need to take this cobbler out the oven so it doesn't burn."

"Okay, just remember what I told you." As I nodded the doorbell rang and Mr. Ben told me he would get it since I was handling the food.

Thankfully, the cobbler had turned out perfect, and as I began to set the plates, I happened to look over at the guest who just walked in. I couldn't believe my eyes—it was Papa Joe. I held my head down so he wouldn't notice me. I couldn't believe it. I never knew that Papa Joe was a wealthy businessman. He lived next door to us, and though we aren't in the poor house, we were nowhere near the status of a wealthy businessman. What was I going to do? If he saw me, I would be embarrassed. I had scarcely seen Papa Joe lately other than when he came over to give us money. I didn't know how he would feel seeing me there. I was afraid he would tell Mr. Ben about the sexual activity we used to engage in with one another. Then I thought maybe somehow Mr. Ben already knew and it influenced the reason that he hired me on. My mind was racing at a thousand miles an hour. Mr. Ben must have somehow noticed my distress because he walked over to me and started talking to me in a whisper again.

"You okay Deborah? You seem like you're in distress?"

"What would make you think that, Mr. Ben?" I said feebly.

"Well the plates are set and yet you're looking under the sink as if you're looking for a pot or something?"

"I'm sorry Mr. Ben, I don't mean to scare you or anything. I'm not ill, I promise. It's just, that man over there."

"Who? You still worried about Evan?"

"No sir, the other one. The one who you just let in," I told him.

"Oh, you mean Joseph? He's a nice guy, did you want me to introduce you to him? Come on." I was going to tell him I already knew him, but Mr. Ben was a very assertive man, and by the time he grabbed my arm and took me to the dining area to introduce me to Papa Joe, it was too late. Papa Joe looked at me and turned beat red

and had a huge smile across his face, the
same one Mr. Ben had when he first met me.

"Debbie? What are you doing here?"
he asked

"You mean you know that nigger?"
Mr. Evan said. Papa Joe looked at Mr. Evan
with fury and said,

"Know her? I damn near raised her!
She and her family stay next to one of the
properties I own."

"You mean the nigger has enough
money to stay near a rich man? That's the
case then why is she working for you Ben?"
Mr. Evan said.

"Ben, who is this man? Are these the
kind of people you're hiring to help run the

company? Do I need to step in and handle hiring?" Papa Joe screamed.

"Joseph I'm sorry, he normally doesn't act like this. Evan will you do us a favor and please excuse yourself since you can't have respect for my employee?" Mr. Ben told him.

"Yeah I'll go, that's quite alright. Just know I still have a say in this company," Mr. Evan said.

"Not anymore, you're fired!" Papa Joe told him.

"You can't just fire me like that, I'm an important member of this company!" Mr. Evan shouted. It almost became violent as they told Mr. Evan to get out, but luckily he left without too much of a hassle. After he was gone, everyone recollected themselves and began returning to the table. I started setting everyone's plates, almost forgetting Papa Joe but I was reminded when they came back to sit down. Papa Joe looked at me as I was finishing setting up everyone's plates and told me to set a plate for myself.

I looked at him and said, "Now that wouldn't be appropriate Papa Joe; this is Mr. Ben's house and I'm just his employee."

"And I'm his boss," he replied sharply. "By extension that makes me your boss as well, so fix yourself a plate and eat with the rest of us."

Mr. Ben looked at me and said, "You heard the man, do as he says". I didn't know what to say, not only were these white men telling me what to do, but they were ordering me to eat with them as if I was one of their own; but I dared not go against their words. I did as they asked, fixed myself a plate, and sat down to eat with them.

Dinner was initially silent, but Papa Joe broke it by asking me,

"So Debbie, when did you start working for Benjamin here? Shouldn't you be in school like your siblings?"

"Today's my first day actually, Papa Joe. Excuse me, Mr. Joseph." I realized it was informal and quite rude to call "Papa Joe" by the name I knew him by while we were at what was supposed to be a business meeting.

"Now Debbie for as long as we've known each other, you should know you don't have to call me "Mr." anything. I'm still Papa Joe to you," he said.

"Yes, sir," I replied.

"You never answered my other question, why aren't you in school?"

"Well, as you know, it's been tough on momma since daddy died. I figured if I went out and got a job then it might benefit the household more than my going to school would."

"If your mother needed more help, all she had to do was ask. Y'all are family to me, you of all people should know that. But I won't go back and forth with you 'bout it. You're a young woman with a good heart and independent spirit, all things that I admire." "Thank you Papa Joe," I told him.

"You're welcome beautiful," he replied with a wink.

After we'd finished talking, you could see the look of curiosity on Mr. Ben's face. It seems as though he had a lot of questions for us about the details of how we knew each other, but he dared not ask Papa Joe, with him being his boss and all. The rest of dinner was eaten with the return of

the previous silence, other than a comment

here and there about how the food tasted, all

positive of course. When we were finished

eating, I began gathering the dishes so I

could clean them, and the three men began

having their meeting in the living room. I

wasn't able to hear their words, not that it

was any of my business anyway since I only

worked for Mr. Ben. But I did notice

something peculiar. Papa Joe kept looking

over at me and giving me a wink and a smile

while I was cleaning. I would just politely

smile back and resume my cleaning.

Honestly, I was still in complete disbelief.

How was it that the man I grew up knowing

and losing my virginity to, ended up being my boss's boss? This was either a clear sign that I belonged at that job or that something about it was going to change my life. At that time I had no clue how true the latter would turn out to be.

The meeting was done about the same time that I was finished cleaning up the kitchen. I was so tired from the dramatic events that occurred, I really didn't want to lift another finger once I was done cleaning. But it wasn't up to me, as Mr. Ben decided when I was to go home. I had heard everyone walking towards the door as Mr. Ben ushered them on their way out. Mr.

William left first, then Papa Joe followed but turned around before he completely exited the house. He looked over Mr. Ben's shoulder and said to me,

"Why don't you ride home with me Debbie? It's too late for a young girl like you to be driving alone."

"Thanks Papa Joe but I'll be fine. The Lord will be with me". He looked as though he was gonna continue to persuade me to ride with him, but Mr. Ben cut in and told him

"My wife's out of town so she'll probably just stay here with me tonight, right Debbie?" He turned and winked his eye at me after saying this and though I was caught off guard, I thought it would be wise to play along.

"Yes sir, that's correct," I told him.

Papa Joe responded, "Well okay, least I can do is let your momma know you're somewhere safe and should be home tomorrow."

"Thank you Papa Joe, I sure do appreciate it." I waved goodbye to him, and Mr. Ben closed the door and began slowly walking towards me. Something about him seemed a bit different as he walked towards me but I thought at first that I was still in shock from seeing Papa Joe. Then, my previous assumption was confirmed when

Mr. Ben stood face to face with me and looked me dead in the eyes and said,

"You are one beautiful negro, you know that?" I didn't know how to respond, I blushed for sure. Mr. Ben was a very attractive man but he had to be at least ten or fifteen years my senior, and he was married. I replied by simply telling him thank you. I'd like to say that it stopped there. He grabbed my hand, stared at me with those piercing blue eyes, and asked me if I had ever been intimate with a man before. I didn't know what to tell him, what kind of question was this to be asked by your employer. My heart began racing and I didn't know what to say or do. He pulled my body even closer to him than I already was and said, "You know, you didn't tell me you knew the boss. If I had known that, I wouldn't have hired you."

"Why not? It's not nepotism if he doesn't know I know you. Plus it's not like he and I are family or anything At least not blood related." He grinned when I said that.

"That's what I like about you, you ain't like most negros. You're intelligent, I caught on to that the moment you came up to my door. You're a beauty to be appreciated". After Mr. Ben said all this, I didn't know whether to be flattered or scared out of my mind. I never liked to make assumptions but it began to remind me of the many experiences I had with Papa Joe since my daddy's parting. Mr. Ben leaned forward and placed his sift red lips against mine. I should have fought back but I gave in, partly out of lust, and partly out of fear of what could happen if I turned him down. His hands then began to move down my thigh and before I knew it, I gave myself to him. We made love all night and it felt different than when I was with Papa Joe. Mr. Ben seemed to know exactly how to please a woman, he was more focused on my satisfaction than his own. What's even stranger is that I felt like an adult that night, not some teenage girl having sneaking around with her next door neighbor. As crazy as it sounds, Mr. Ben made me feel loved, more loved than I had felt since my father died. But despite all of that, I shouldn't have done it. I opened a doorway for him that I don't think ever closed, even now long after he's gone. He made an imprint on my soul that was always leave me hungry for him. I will always remember that day as both magical and one of the biggest mistakes I've made in my entire life.

CHAPTER FOUR

As the months went by, I began to work for Mr. Ben more, eventually working every day. He always appreciated my work and the other things that I kept offering to him. I would see his wife come and go for days at time but he never seem affected when she was there. He hardly paid her any attention if I'm being honest, but he did love his kids. You can tell he really enjoyed the thought of being a father because he was overjoyed when his kids came back home. He played with them, helped them with their homework during the school season, and spent all his time with them during the summertime. As much as I hate admitting it, this is one of the reasons that my feelings for Mr. Ben grew exponentially. I always admired a man who was good with kids because I had wanted to be a parent myself one day, especially since my daddy's passing. Of course Mr. Ben didn't know any of that and I wouldn't have dared to tell him as I didn't want him to think I had any interest in replacing his wife.

One day while I was cleaning and Mr. Ben was out playing 'round with the farm animals and his kids, his wife walked up to me.

"Deborah, may I talk to you for a minute?" I began to get nervous. What if she had found out about the secret affair that I had been carrying on with her husband? What would she do to me, fire me? Kill me? I had little time to process my anxious thoughts and had to push past them so I wouldn't come off suspicious.

"Why of course," I said anxiously. She led me to the sofa and told me to take a seat. She looked outside to make sure Mr. Ben and the kids were plenty busy so they wouldn't interrupt us. She then walked back towards the sofa with her blood red lipstick, sparkling blue dress, and curly brown hair and sat next to me.

"Well first off, I know we hardly ever talk, so I wanted to take some time to do that." Her opening statement was a red flag alone. It wasn't just that we "hardly ever talked" as she so kindly put it, we actually never talked before. Even when she and the kids first came back, she pulled Mr. Ben aside and I could hear him telling her in a whisper that he had hired me to help around and such. After that she would just look at me, and even when she needed me to get something and Mr. Ben wasn't around, she would send one of the kids to ask for her. I guess she thought that she was too good to talk to negros.

"No mam, we don't talk much but I'm usually working and you seem like you're always busy tending to your family so I don't take it personally." She gave a slight smile, almost like it made her feel good that I exaggerated the attention she showed to her children and husband.

"Well thank you for saying that Deborah. But that gives me no excuse to be rude, especially not to such a young beautiful girl as yourself." I was told that often by them, I think they thought I was the most beautiful creature God had created. I guess it's because I looked so different from them. She continued, "Benjamin tells me you've stayed

the night here before when I'm not home?"
Anxiously, I told her,

"Yes mam, it's happened a few times when I would work late."

"There's no need to explain yourself, I just wanted to ask you a question."

"Okay," I said. "Ask away."

"Well before I ask you this, I want you to know that this stays strictly between us girls. You can tell me the truth and no matter what you say, I won't let you lose your job with us, knowing how important this job is to you." I became nervous, my heart was thumping so loud in my chest that I was afraid she might be able to hear it and would become even more suspicious, although if she was about to ask what I was thinking, then it was already too late for me. "When you turn in at night, do you ever notice Benjamin leaving the house?"

"No ma'am, it always seems quiet to me," I told her. She stared at me for a minute before replying.

"Okay, that's all I wanted to know. Thank you Deborah. " She got up from the couch and began walking upstairs towards the bedroom. I don't know what made me do what I did next, but I couldn't help myself.

"Mrs. Smith?" I said as she turned around to look at me with an eyebrow raised. "Mr. Ben loves you." She looked at me for a minute and replied,

"Thank you Deborah, it means a lot to hear you say that. Benjamin speaks very highly of you, you are more than an employee to him. You are a friend. I say this to say I trust what you're telling me is true. I won't ask for the details though." She smiled at me as she continued walking upstairs. I was speechless, I couldn't believe that she thought Mr. Ben was stepping out on her. I mean she wasn't wrong, but what she didn't realize is that the person he was cheating on her with is the same person that she just said she trusted. What struck me as odd though is that she wasn't the least bit suspicious about Mr. Ben speaking highly of me, but perhaps it was because I was a negro, and she never expected him to be attracted to someone like me.

I spent the rest of that day more focused on finishing my job and getting home as quickly as I could. The last thing I wanted to do was anything that would throw her suspicions towards me. I tried to rush out at around 10:00 P.M but Mr. Ben stopped me before I could get to my car. "Deborah, can we talk for a minute?" he asked.

"Sure Mr. Ben, but I am in a bit of a rush" I told him.

"It'll only be a minute," he said as he closed the door, leaving us standing on the front porch alone. "Earlier I noticed my wife talking to you. Did she say anything out of the ordinary?"

I hesitated to tell him but I couldn't hide anything from him. "Well now that you mention it, yes. She asked if I had heard you going anywhere on the nights that I stay here and she's out of town with the kids," I explained.

"Is that right? And what did you tell her?"

"Well, I told her that I never hear you leave your room and that you really love her."

"Well I'll be damned, you are not only a great cook and an excellent cleaner, but you're also loyal. All the more reason for me ask you this: would you like to move in with us?"

"What? Move in? Mr. Ben, what about my family? I can't just leave them, I'm the main breadwinner. What am I supposed to tell my momma?"

"I know it's a bit confusing but I talked it over with my wife and she agrees that you would benefit well from living with us. And of course I sure would appreciate it on a personal level," he told me as he stroked my puffy afro hair. He continued, "It will be a five cent pay raise, and it's not like you'll be locked inside the house. You'll be free to go and see your family whenever you want, that way you can still help your momma out and save up some money on the side in case you want a place of your own one day."

He was very convincing, Mr. Ben always had a way with his words. "Well you do make a good point, I'll be close to you and able to better provide for you and your family," I told him.

"Tell you what, why don't you give it some thought and get back to me whenever you decide. I don't mean to pressure you but it would increase our time together and you know how much I value that. I suspect that you do too."

I replied, "You're suspicions are right, and because of that I don't need any time. I'll do it, I'll move in with you." I couldn't believe what I had just agreed to, it was the same feeling that I had when I just willingly made love to him. It was this irresistible attraction about Mr. Ben that I simply could not get away from or say no to. He was so happy when I said yes that he leapt towards me and kissed me in a moment of impulse. After he realized what he just did, he tried to play it off and wave me goodbye as I got into my car. I blew a kiss to him as I drove off into the night.

I couldn't believe it, not only was I moving out of my house but I was moving in with a man I was having an affair with. It felt so wrong but so right at the same time. If I had any sense at that time, I would have paid attention to the deep feeling of dread I felt deep down on the inside, but I was too caught up in my emotions to even acknowledge it. I knew that this was about more than a five cents raise on my part, it was about something deeper though I'm not exactly sure what. It was something that I couldn't really put my finger on or put a name to. Love, maybe? Perhaps, I did love Mr. Ben but I don't think that's the only force behind my irresistible attraction to Mr.

Ben. Instead of trying to figure it out, I figured it was just be best to take it all while I can.

The next day I had a talk with my mother early in the morning about my decision to move in with Mr. Ben, and she didn't even bother fighting me on it. I knew that my mother had a love for me as her daughter, but she knew I was too independent and quite frankly making too much money for her to disagree with. My siblings, on the other hand, tried to fight me on my decision. They brought up how I wouldn't be doing any of this if daddy was around—and they were right. If my father had still been alive then I wouldn't be doing any of these things, I'd be going to school and driving out to the country with him to get some fresh produce for the house. But the reality was that my father was gone, so I had to move on with my life. I tried to make them understand, but all they could say is I was wrong and that living with a white man and his family was only dangerous. I heard their words and appreciated their concern, but it didn't matter to me, I'd made up my mind. I was moving out and that was final.

As I packed my suitcases in my car, I noticed Papa Joe was peeking out the window from his living room at me. He didn't know about my decision at that time. I hadn't told him and given our history, and had no intention of doing so. I was too afraid that if I did, he might try to go after Mr. Ben on the account of being jealous that I would be staying with him. He walked out his front door and began approaching me as I entered the car. I tried to start it up and act like I didn't see him but he got to me before I could pull off. He practically ran over to the car and motioned for me to let my window down. I reluctantly did, and he asked,

"Well where are you in a rush off to? Taking a vacation from Benjamin?"

I replied, "Actually, I'm moving in with Mr. Ben to better tend to him and his family's needs." Papa Joe's face dropped. It was like someone just drove a nail through his heart.

"M-moving in with B-Benjamin? W-what made that h-happen?"

"Well, he had a talk with his wife and with her going out of town and all, they figured it would benefit them well if I moved in." Papa Joe stared at me before replying. His look was a mixture of disappointment and slight curiosity. Then, still not responding, he walked over to my passenger door, opened it, and let himself in. He pulled out a match and lit a cigarette, then told me to let my window up, which I found strange but was obedient to regardless.

"You aren't fucking him, are you?" I didn't know what to say. I never heard Papa Joe talk to me like that before. He was always nice and treated me with respect. Before I could respond, he took a puff of his cigarette and continued "cause if you are and you end up carrying his child, I'll make sure you regret it." I couldn't believe it, the man who had been like a father figure to me my whole life had threatened me. Because he was also my boss, I really didn't know what to say.

I finally got the courage to say something after a minute or two of complete shock. "Papa Joe, I was raised to be a woman. It wouldn't be lady-like for me to sleep with another woman's husband would it? Not to mention, he's my boss. Now what kind of employee sleeps with their own boss?" I told him. I knew that what I said sounded exactly like what it was—complete bullcrap—but I had to say something. He took another puff of his cigarette and looked at me in the eyes and said,

"Debbie, you're a beautiful girl but you're lying through your teeth. I know from what you did with me that you have favor for white men, and Benjamin ain't no run of the mill bullhonkey. He's attractive and well established. But you listen to me, you get caught doing something with him and that will not only be the end of your employment, but also the end of his. I will tell him about the deeds you did with me and how I'm the one who took your virginity from you. Now I don't reckon he would like hearing that, would he?" I didn't respond. He continued "I know you think I sound hateful right now but I assure you this is for your own good. It's one thing to mess around with me 'cause I know you, but you don't know Benjamin. This man would throw you out if he ever knew the truth of what you've done with me or God knows how many other white men you've been with. So I tell you this not as a threat but as a warning, be careful. One wrong step can turn your whole life around and I know your momma would hate to hear that her daughter lost her job from screwing with her boss. Now, I have a personal property you can stay on if leaving home is all you want to do. Nobody has to know you're there but you and me. You can quit your job with Benjamin and work for me directly. You know I'm not married and sure would appreciate your service." I was distraught, I couldn't believe what was being said to me in that moment. I had a choice to either move in with the man I had begun to fall in love with, but risk the possibility of losing it all by a man I knew and loved as a father figure my whole life; or, I could go to work for that father figure, have my own place, probably be paid better, but lose what I had with Mr. Ben. It was a hard decision, I won't lie. I weighed my options out in my head for what seemed like hours, and then turned to Papa Joe.

"I love you Papa Joe, you are the closest thing I've had to a dad since daddy passed away. But I am not guilty of anything except being a good employee for Mr. Ben and doing as he instructed me to do. With that said, I'm gonna have to turn down your offer and stay working for Mr. Ben. I sure do appreciate you looking out for me though." He took a final puff of what little of the cigarette remained from our conversation, opened the car door and began to get out. Then, before he closed it, he looked at me and said,

"I damn sure hope you're telling the truth, Debbie, 'cause if I found out you aren't, your blood will be on your own hands." He closed the car door gently after that and walked away from me, looking back one final time as if to let me know the offer was still open. I turned on my car and drove off as fast as I could so he would get the message. I was not only hurt beyond words but I was furious with Papa Joe for threatening me. I wanted him dead in that moment but what I didn't realize then was in his own selfish way, Papa Joe was actually trying to save me.

When I arrived at Mr. Ben's place, my new home, I noticed his wife's car was gone. I couldn't help but think deep down that he had somehow planned for that to happen. He must have been standing by the front door waiting on me, 'cause as soon as I arrived, he rushed outside and gave me a big hug and kissed me.

"Welcome home, honey." It felt good hearing those words, like I really had found somewhere I belonged and someone I had been longing for. He helped me get my things inside and I don't know if it was the summer heat getting to us or what, but we quickly jumped in bed together like a couple of jack rabbits. We made love for hours, I didn't want it to ever end. In between our love making, we would just lie there and chat about life and how good it was to finally be able to be with one another full time(until his wife came home of course.) In the middle of us talking, Papa Joe somehow came up in the conversation. I can't remember which one of us brought him up, but I didn't tell him about what Papa Joe threatened me with. I was too afraid that if I told him then it would have ruined everything. Looking back now, it might have changed some things if I had told him.

The next few weeks were a dream come true, even the days when his wife was there. We would sneak out to the barns and make love like a couple of teenagers. One thing our relationship was never built off of: fear. We were never afraid of getting caught. One night when I had finished cooking and cleaning and making sure all the kids were in bed, I heard whispers coming from outside. I knew for sure that Mr. Ben was in bed because I had personally made sure he was. But I hadn't seen his wife since before dinner; seemed like she just disappeared. Mr. Ben wasn't too concerned about her of course because less time with her meant more time with me, but I am a very analytical person. Something in my body felt strange about her not being there, especially after hearing those whispers coming from outside.

When I looked out the curtain in the living room I noticed Papa Joe talking to Mr. Ben's wife. I couldn't hear what they were saying but judging from her reaction, it wasn't anything good. She covered her mouth and began crying, then he comforted her, wrapping his arms around her. I couldn't believe it, did Papa Joe just snitch on me like he threatened he would? Why would he do this to me? I was so furious that I almost grabbed a knife and walked out the house to show him what happens to white men who go around blathering secrets to people. But, I'm glad I didn't because what happened next threw me completely off. Papa Joe grabbed Mr. Ben's wife and began kissing her. I couldn't believe it. The same man who was warning and threatening me about infidelity was now committing it with Mr. Ben's wife of all people. A part of me was upset that he would do that to Mr. Ben, who was both his friend and his employee, but another part of me was happy. I had some kind of leverage to use against him. Before I could close the curtain all the way, he happened to look up and caught a glimpse of me. I began rushing upstairs until I realized I had nothing to be afraid of; the power was now in my hands any way. So I turned around and went back to the kitchen just in time to see Mr. Ben's wife and Papa Joe entering the house. They both looked at me suspiciously.

"Shouldn't you be in bed, Deborah?" she said sternly.

"Yes mam, I was just finishing up the kitchen."

"Looks pretty clean to me. Now why don't you get yourself to bed before you get in all kinds of trouble? A servant needs her rest," she said in the most condescending voice.

"Couldn't agree more Mrs. Smith. But before I go, did you want me to get Mr. Ben?"

"Excuse me?" She looked like she wanted to choke me to death and rightfully so, I knew my offer would make her uncomfortable. "I just figured since Papa Joe was here, he was about to have a late night business meeting with Mr. Ben."

Her expression relaxed as she realized that her previous reaction might have hinted at her guilty nature. "Oh no, I mean Mr. Joseph is here to meet with me. We have some business to discuss, just between us." I gave her a fake smile and she returned it

Goodnight to you and Papa Joe then, enjoy your meeting"

"That's Mr. Joseph to you." Those words broke my heart and I'm not even sure why. It felt like a man that I had so much history with suddenly treated me like I was akin to being one of his slaves. I didn't want to show this vulnerability in front of him or arouse any suspicion in Mr. Ben's wife so I simply nodded my head as I walked up the stairs and went to my bedroom. As I got into bed, all I kept thinking was Papa Joe with Mr. Ben's wife. How was I gonna tell Mr. Ben about it? Would he even believe me? Those thoughts swirled around in my mind as I tossed and turned trying to get some rest. After a while, I finally began dozing off, but just then I heard a small knock and heard footsteps coming in the room. I didn't know what to say, it was too dark for me to see who it was and I had my back turned away from the side of the room the door was on. I didn't want to say anything too quickly, assuming it was Mr. Ben. It couldn't have been him any way, it was too late and too risky for him to come in my room at this time of the night. I didn't have much time to decide if I was going to play possum, because I felt a hand touch me. It was Mr. Ben, I knew that touch anywhere. He kissed me on the forehead and got in bed with me. I didn't say a word to him, didn't have any time to because he laid his lips on mine and before I knew it we were kissing and I was getting ready to pull my clothes off. Then, he spoke and my heart sank to the bottom of my chest. "God it feels good to kiss you again, Debbie. It's been too long". That voice wasn't Mr. Ben. It was Papa Joe.

I had half a mind to ball my fist up and hit him to get him the hell off of me. But as he was pushing his weight on me, he whispered in my ear words that I'll never forget.

"Now you're gonna give me what you've been giving to Benjamin. I've known you your whole life and I'm not gonna let you mess it up by getting involved with any other man than myself. See I promised your dad that I would take care of you and that's exactly what I intend to do." He was delusional, I couldn't believe Papa Joe was like that. All I kept thinking to myself how could I get out of this. I didn't want to just give myself to him when I had dedicated my body and my heart to Mr. Ben. I didn't want to give myself to Papa Joe but I had no way to fight him off, the only thing I could think was to scream for help. Papa Joe must have known that ran across my mind because as he kept kissing me and while I tried to resist him, he spoke again in my ear. "I know what you're thinking, you wanna call for his help, don't you? Well if you do, think about what he will say. He'll know someone had to let me in the house, and he knows his wife would never do such a thing. So the choice is yours Debbie, either give yourself to me willingly or scream and ruin both of our lives." He was right, I was stuck. If I screamed for help, it would cause nothing but trouble. Papa Joe could fire Mr. Ben, Mr. Ben wouldn't know whether to believe I let Papa Joe in or not and his wife, God only knows what his wife would say to turn it all on me. It was pointless in fighting it; he had won. So I gave myself to him. As disgusted and repulsed as I was, I did it. I remember everything about that moment, the way Papa Joe smelled like an old sweaty man, how I felt so weak and powerless because of my inability to overpower him, and how the darkness made it all seem like a nightmare, one I was swallowed up in.

When he was finished he kissed me once more and said I was a good girl for not screaming. He ran his fingers across my hair and said that he loved me, that although I probably hated him, he loved me. He then laid there for a moment on top of me, and as much as I hate to say it, it brought some sense of comfort that I still don't understand. In a way it felt comforting to know that he didn't just want to use my body and discard me, he held me like I was his daughter, like he really loved me. I may not have wanted him to but I really didn't have much of a choice, physically or emotionally. I ended up falling asleep and only woke when he was getting ready to leave. I didn't know what time it was, nor did I really care, I just wanted him gone. He didn't know I was awake as he got himself together and walked towards the door. I heard him murmur under his breath that he was sorry before, then he opened the door as silently as he could and walked out, closing it in the same manner he opened it. I just laid there for a minute and stared into the darkness thinking of everything that had happened since my father died. It was like every victory I tried to get came with a trade-off in some way. I just couldn't win. My eyes began welling up with tears as uncontrollable thoughts crossed my mind, I just wanted to escape. I felt like a used up washcloth that had been squeezed until it was completely dry. I hated myself, I needed a way out of this situation, out of everything. But I didn't see a way out, I didn't think there was one. It's like I was trapped in my own hell and there was no chance for redemption. Then, just when I thought things couldn't get any worse, I heard an abrupt knock on my door and before I could respond I heard Mr. Ben calling my name in the most aggressive tone I've ever heard him talk in. He ordered me to meet him downstairs immediately slammed the door on the way out. What could he have wanted? There's no way Papa Joe went back and told him what had just happened between us It would not only destroy my relationship but also his with Mr. Ben's wife. Then again, I don't think he cared much for her if he was so desperate to come after me. I had no time to play the guessing game so I slipped on my clothes and hurried downstairs. I froze. Papa Joe was sitting there in the living room with Mr. Ben and his wife. I walked up to them, quaking with fear. Mr. Ben ordered me to sit down right next to Papa Joe, right across from him and his wife. I sat down and Papa Joe grabbed my hand. I tried to pull away but his grip was too strong.

Mr. Ben's wife began the conversation. "I know that you are staying with us, Deborah, and I think I speak for me and Benjamin when I say we appreciate all your hard work."

"Thank you" I told her nervously.

"And with your hard work," she continued, as if she didn't hear me, "we understand that you're interested in having a personal life. But for you to not only bring another man in this house without permission, but also sleep with the boss is very—"

"It's goddamn disrespectful that's what it is," Mr. Ben cut in. "We have sacrificed everything for you, let you move in here, eat with us, take care of our kids, and this is how you repay us! What was the reason!? Was I not paying you enough!? Or maybe you thought you would move up further in the company by sleeping with the boss? So what is it, huh?" I had never heard Mr. Ben yell like this before. He was furious, he was hurt. His face was beet red and he kept concealing tears from coming out. His wife just looked at Papa Joe like she wanted to kill him. I didn't respond, I didn't know what I could say. I couldn't plead my case before everybody and expose Mr.

Ben's and my relationship, but I couldn't

explain what Papa Joe threatened either.

Once again, I was stuck... Mr. Ben was

furious at my silence and marched towards

me. "Answer me you cotton-picking

nigger!" He raised his hand and was about to

hit me until Papa Joe stopped him. They

stared at one another for a minute, then Mr.

Ben said he was going to bed and walked

away. His wife followed him, leaving me

and Papa Joe on the sofa.

Papa Joe looked at me as I sat there

in tears, shaking from the hit I almost got

from the man I loved. He said, "Come on

Debbie, we should go," as he extended his

hand to assist me. I wanted to chop his hand

off, the hand that was responsible for all of it. I almost attacked him until I heard Mr. Ben coming back downstairs, this time by himself. He looked at me with the greatest conviction and said,

"As of tonight, you can consider yourself no longer my employee. Now take your shit and get out of my house." That was it, the relationship, my fantasy, it was all over. If I had any time to explain myself, I would have. But the best thing I could do at this point was take Papa Joe's hand and follow orders. So I did, and we got all of my things and left. The life that I had spent so much time building with Mr. Ben was over. It was time for me to move on to something

else. I didn't have much of a choice, I
wanted to plead his forgiveness, ask him to
have mercy on me. But what could I do? He
didn't want to hear a thing I had to say, Papa
Joe had launched a full scale plan to get me
and it seemed to work out in his favor. And
what could I do? I hadn't saved up enough
money to get a place of my own since I was
still supporting momma and the family, and
I damn sure couldn't stay out on the street
by myself. So I went with Papa Joe, I was in
bondage to him, he had power over me. He
fought for me and without my say so, he had
won.

CHAPTER FIVE

I spent the next few years of my life working for and eventually raising a family with Papa Joe. Shortly after I left Mr. Ben's house, I found out I was pregnant. I didn't know who the father was but I was with Papa Joe, Joseph as I started calling him, and he was all too willing to raise a family with me. During my time with him, he treated me surprisingly well. He realized that everything he did to get me was wrong and would spend every day apologizing to me and trying to make it up to me. If I'm being honest, I was somewhat grateful for what he did. I had no business messing around with another woman's husband and all he wanted was to see me happy. I recalled when he told me that I didn't know Mr. Ben that well and he turned out to be right. I never thought he would call me a nigger or raise his hand to hit me, especially when I had no chance to explain myself. I knew that although I loved Mr. Ben with all my heart, what we had was wrong from the beginning. What I had with Papa Joe made more sense. Sure he was a bit older than Mr. Ben but he knew me like the back of his hand. He treated me like I was worth something, like I really meant something to him. I had told momma about us being together after about a year or so, and she was supportive. Back in those days, it wasn't uncommon for a young black woman to be with an older white man. It was something that had been established in our bloodline tracing back to the days of slavery. Don't misunderstand me, what I had with Joseph was not slavery, although it may have looked like it to some. It was a life that I built for myself in accordance with the decisions that I had made since my father died. It was a life that I could honestly say I was happy with.

After a few years of being together and having three kids, Joseph began to grow terminally ill. He was having all sorts of health issues and taking care of him had become similar to taking care of the other kids. I didn't mind of course, I really cared about him. But with his condition, our life as a couple had slowly come to an end. He told me I was much too young to be dealing with an old man and not living my life to the fullest. He also warned me that he would probably be passing away soon. When he said it, I didn't want to believe it. But I knew that if I started accepting it now then it would hurt a lot less when it really did happen. It wouldn't be my like my father's death, abrupt and unexpected. He gave me permission to start dating other people and I did as he requested. I had met this fine young light-skinned man at the grocery store and I instantly felt attracted to him. He approached me while I was getting some things for the house, what little things we didn't have already.

"Excuse me miss. If you don't mind me saying, you are stunning." His pickup line wasn't the best, but I figured I'd entertain him.

"Well I appreciate you saying that, you ain't so bad yourself." I told him.

"If you really think so, then why don't you go on a date with me this weekend? Maybe I can take you out and show you a good time." I didn't want to seem desperate but I wanted to leap when he asked me that. But I couldn't let him think he had power over me. So I played hard-to-get.

"Well you gotta do a little better than that if you want me to go out with you. I mean you didn't even tell me your name, don't you have any manners?" I asked him.

"I apologize, my name is Benjamin James but you can call me Ben." I couldn't believe it, God had brought me another Ben. I didn't mean to sound so superstitious but it felt like God had somehow moved mountains in my life for that very moment. I could finally be with another Benjamin, I just hoped that he wasn't married. Turned out he wasn't and we went on a date that weekend. And that was only one of many dates that we went on. It was a bit of a struggle trying to date, taking care of an ill individual, and raising three kids, but I managed to pull it off. I always was an independent woman, so I was used to having many things to do at once.

It wasn't long into dating Ben that Joseph passed away. I was hurt but having Benjamin there, plus my kids, helped me get through it. They grieved at losing their dad at such a young age, but we gave him a real nice funeral. My oldest was about eight years old at that point, just a few years younger than I was when I lost my father. I did my best to console him through it and be the mother that he needed. I talked to him, comforted him, did everything I could to make sure he and his siblings knew that I loved them more than anything and would be with them throughout the entire grieving process. Benjamin stepped in and stepped up as well and I can't tell you how much I appreciated him being there for support. It wasn't the financial support I needed (Joseph had left me and the kids a nice inheritance we were surviving off of and I was working part-time taking care of an older white woman.) But Benjamin gave us rivers of living water. We had a friend, a husband, a father, everything. Ben was truly my dream come true and now that Papa Joe was no longer around, I knew I needed to do something to represent the new life I'd been quickly building with Benjamin.

After about a year after Papa Joe's death, I became pregnant with my fourth child. I was thrilled because this would be my first child with Benjamin. I said to myself that I wanted things to be a bit different with this child though. I wanted this child to see what it was like to not only see his or her parents happy together, but also to be able to say their parents are married. When I had gotten home from work one day, I told Benjamin to sit down so I could have a talk with him. I told him that he'd been so great with me and the kids and I just wanted him to know how much I truly appreciated him and wanted him in my life. I then proceeded to ask him if he would marry me. He laughed.

"Either you've been spying on me the whole time you've been at work, or The Lord Himself has been speaking to you."

"What do you mean?" I replied.

"This," he said as he went into his pocket and pulled out the most beautiful ring I had ever seen in my life. He got down on one knee and said, "Deborah, will you marry me?" I shouted to the high heavens and told him yes. It was the most joyous I had ever been my whole life. The man I had met a little over a year ago ended up being the man that I would spend the rest of my life with. It was the turnaround that Christians shout about in church and pray about getting. The Lord had not only heard my prayers, but He opened the windows of Heaven and let His glorious light shine down upon me.

Ben and I still hadn't set a wedding date because we were so busy preparing for the birth of our baby; but we did want to get married before she was born. I had already decided on what her name would be: Michelle James. I couldn't wait, there was just something so special about having a child with Ben. Don't get me wrong, I loved all my kids equally. But there is nothing like having a child with a person that you are truly in love with, a feeling that's inexpressible. Ben and I took a drive out of the state one weekend with the kids so we could spend some family time together. I told him that I had always wanted to travel but was just too afraid or too busy to do so on my own. Prior to him coming in my world, my whole life was a constant process of taking care of people that I lived with, moving out of their house and into a new situation, and then realizing that my new situation was just a repeat of my old situation except with different people. Ben helped me somehow get free from that process, those chains of bondage no longer had anymore hold on me. He drove us to a place in Florida, a small town called Pensacola. He had family there and said that he wanted me to see how special of a town it was. I'll admit, I was a bit nervous about meeting one of his family members, because up 'til that point, I had not even met his mother. Back in those days, meeting someone's mother was a determining factor in the future of the relationship. If the parent's didn't like you, then it would be difficult for them to hand over their child to you. I introduced him to my mother and she didn't say much about him other than that she hoped I was making the right decision by bringing him in my life. But I wasn't too concerned about her ambivalence because she and I weren't very close at that point. Between me going through everything I had been through and not having time to keep in touch with her, we drifted apart. She was upset that she barely got a chance to see her grandkids and told me my siblings wished I would make some effort to include them in my life. What I couldn't get my mother to understand though is that I purposely distanced myself from them, being around my family only reminded me of my past and everything that I lost with the passing of my dad. However I didn't know how close Benjamin was with his mother and was very concerned as to what she may think of me. I just wanted everything with Ben to be perfect, I wanted nothing to get in the way of our beautiful love story.

When we arrived in Pensacola, we immediately went to someone's house that Ben said was his cousin. I felt a little less nervous about meeting him but at least it wasn't his mother. His cousin was very sweet and welcoming, (though he seemed a bit strange to me, but I chalked that up to him being from a different state.) He had a huge house, which struck me as odd being that he didn't seem to have a wife or any kids around. This kind of reminded me of Mr. Ben since that's how he usually lived his life, big empty house that he kept to himself mostly. But, who was I to judge? I didn't even know the man after all. He and Benjamin were the best of friends, I could tell how much they missed each other. They hugged, were very chummy with each other, and it was nice to see two men showing such affection towards one another. It wasn't something I was accustomed to since I had never seen my dad get very affectionate with anyone except me. It was about evening time and I went to lie down and let Ben and his cousin have their alone time, since I could see how much they wanted to catch back up with each other, but also because the baby kept kicking me . All the kids were in their own rooms taking a nap. As I was lying down, I was thinking about how far God had brought me over the years and just started praising Him and thanking Him. He had been so good to me despite everything that I had been through. My life was becoming a true story of redemption, almost worthy of being in The Bible, or at least I thought so. When I was done, I had begun nodding off to sleep, but was awaken when I heard a faint noise coming from the living room. I thought that maybe it was just Ben and his cousin being young men and rough housing with one another. But I wanted to check on them and make sure everything was alright. As I walked out the room, trying to be as quiet as possible, I tiptoed down the hallway that lead into the living room. The noise that was going on kept getting louder and my anxiety began to shoot through the roof even more than when Mr. Ben called me downstairs that day I lost my job. But, I tried my best to keep calm by telling myself that it was all in my imagination and that I was somehow just having hallucinations while I was pregnant. Then, as I peeped around the corner, I saw something that tore my heart out of my chest.

Benjamin and his so called "cousin" were on the couch having sex with one another! My heart sank, I must have been dreaming. This wasn't real, not my Benjamin, not the same man whose baby I was carrying. It wasn't possible that he could be queer. I knew I wasn't no man, and he had shown me so much attention when my clothes were off that I knew it just couldn't be real. I quickly closed my eyes and tried to walk away, hoping to wake up from what I assumed was just a nightmare. In my stupidity and desperation, I walked back towards the corner to confirm if what I had just seen was real. It was. There they were, kissing on one another and giving their bodies to each other in the most offensive manner. There was no hesitation on either end, nothing was forced or anything of the sort. What killed me is that Benjamin looked at the man like he looked at me. He looked at him like he had real feelings for him, like he could have…could have been in love with him. All I could do was burst into tears. My dream had come to an end, once again I had not left behind the pain of my past. I had only escaped from one situation to the next.

The worst part about it is that I had no one to run to. Papa Joe was gone and Ben was all I had. I damn sure couldn't go back to my mom's house and tell her I left my fiancé because he slept with a man. And Mr. Ben was way out of the equation. So, I stood there feeling sorry for myself for a few minutes until I noticed the noise had stopped. They were finished and were kissing and holding one another. I needed to go back to the room, but the moment I turned around, the baby kicked me so hard that I made a noise as I almost fell to my knees.

The last thing I wanted was Benjamin seeing me spying on him, even if he was in the wrong. I tried to get up quickly but before I did, I heard footsteps coming around the corner and Benjamin talking. "Is someone there? Hello? Deborah is that you?" His voice boomed through the hallway and right down into the pit of my stomach. What was I going to do? I kept trying to think of something quick but every time I tried to move, the baby kept kicking. It had to be the worst luck I had ever had, and I was considering changing that baby's name to Ichabod because I felt that the presence of The Lord had departed from me. Just when I thought that, God showed me that He was still with me. The footsteps began to turn around and I heard them getting further away. I didn't know what made him change his mind about coming around that corner but I was damn glad that he did. I was finally able to get up and stagger my way back towards the bedroom. I laid down but couldn't get back to sleep, who would be able to after seeing what I saw? I started thinking to myself about how I could address what I had just seen with Ben, but I only kept seeing myself handling the situation in a way that I didn't want to. I kept thinking that maybe I should just take the kids and leave, we could go back to Alabama and let Benjamin figure out on his own why I left. But I couldn't do that to him, for one we stayed together so he would eventually get back home and I'd have to explain why I left. My other option was to just break up with him, call the wedding and everything off. I had plenty of money after all and Papa Joe wouldn't want me being with someone that didn't truly love me. But it was that thought that helped me make up my mind, I couldn't leave him. Despite what I had just experienced, I knew that the way Ben felt about me was something real. I knew it was something that I would regret letting go of. At that time we had no awareness of terms like bisexual like we do today but I convinced myself that maybe Ben just liked men and women. Maybe he felt like that for a very long time and didn't know how to express it. I was rationalizing of course, I was well aware of that, but it didn't mean that I was wrong. There was only one way to know that if what I was telling myself was true, I just had to ask Benjamin if it was. He might feel uncomfortable with me asking but it's better than me just sitting in silence and suffering. I had to ask him to know the truth.

Later that night, we were still at the guy's house. His name was Lonnie, I refused to refer to him as Benjamin's cousin after that because I knew for a fact that he couldn't have been. What kind of person would something like that with their own family member? Despite what some people think about southerners, we aren't a bunch of hillbillies that like to participate in incest. At about nine or ten o'clock, Benjamin came in the bedroom and laid down beside me. He began holding me and asked "are you okay? You've been in bed the whole day?" He knew how much I liked to stay active. I told him I was experiencing some pain from the baby. He offered me some dinner that he and Lonnie had cooked but I wasn't too interested in eating it. That surprised him because it was my favorite: fried mullet and collard greens cooked with some neck bones. Usually I would have given anything to eat that on any day of the week but how was I supposed to eat knowing what I knew? Benjamin knew too that something wasn't right because he asked me "what's going on

Deb? Talk to me." I knew that if I didn't get it out then it was going to eat me from the inside out and since I had no interest in having an emotional tapeworm inside my body, I turned towards him and was blunt with him.

"Earlier I heard a noise in the living room and decided to see what it was. When I got there I saw… I saw you and your… you and Lonnie making love on the couch." He grew quiet, he didn't say a word or make a sound. And his quietness made me think that maybe I really shouldn't have said anything. He looked at the wall and just tapped his index finger on his knee. I'd never seen him do anything like that before and it scared me half to death. But I'm glad I said something to him because I knew this problem had to be addressed, "if you like men Ben, you can tell me. I won't judge you or tell anyone about it, it'll be our little secret. I promise you, I won't say a" before I could get my last words out he grabbed me by the throat and stared at me with his pupils so black you would have thought a demon possessed him.

"Listen Deborah, what you saw out there is none of your damn business. You're a woman and you need to stay in a woman's place. That means shutting your mouth and doing what your husband tells you to do, understand?" I nodded my head out of fear and desperation. His grip was so tight on me that I couldn't even think about breathing. The tone in his voice alone was enough to make even the toughest man quiver in fear like a helpless child. Thankfully, he eased his grip up on me and eventually let go. He walked out the room after that without saying another word. I just sat there on the bed, speechless. I didn't have anything else to say, according to him, I shouldn't say anything anyway. I felt like doing the only thing I knew how to do when things became that bad— praying. But for some reason, my body wouldn't let me. I felt frozen in time, like everything around me stopped and I could do nothing to make time start again. The hopeless feeling of dread that I felt when Papa Joe had forced himself on me at Mr. Ben's house returned. So I told myself I had to be okay with everything. What else could I do? I couldn't pray. I couldn't breathe. I could barely even think. So I had to act like none of what had just happened affected me and I just needed to move on from it. With that thought in mind, that's what I did. I moved on from the situation like it never happened.

Over the next few days, I had a chance to meet the other members of the family. Ben's mom was a sweet, quiet woman. She treated me like I was one of her own, something I appreciated very much. I talked to her and asked her a few questions about Ben.

"If you don't my asking, what was Ben like as a kid?"

"He was good, never was one to get into much trouble. Out of all my children, he was by far the smartest and the most handsome. He stayed to himself a lot though, it was difficult to get him out of the house. He was always into things that most kids his age weren't into." "Such as what?"

"Well, he liked to fix cars for one. Every single time we would have an issue with a car we had, he always volunteered to figure it out."

"That's quite amazing for a kid, I know Ben is smart but I never knew to what extent."

"Benjamin was a bonafide genius, anything you gave him he could fix it. Watches, toys, everything. I remember this one time when he was a teenager he built this electronic toy, shaped like a box, he said one day people all over the world would own one. He had big ambitions, even at 13 or 14 years old. One thing about him is that he was not much into dating. Every child is different of course and he would occasionally bring his friends over the house, both female and male. But he just never struck me as the dating type, guess he just wanted to wait until he met the right person."

She chuckled after saying that but I didn't find it very amusing for some reason. If anything it struck my curiosity as to why he would even be interested in me, obviously I wasn't "the one" he was waiting for because he couldn't even stay committed to me.

"Could you maybe elaborate a little more on that if you don't mind? You never saw Benjamin date anyone at all as a teenager?"

"Isn't much to elaborate on. He had his interest and girls were not on his mind during that period in his life. You have three children so I'm sure you understand how different some kids can be."

"You're right, all of my kids are very different. I do have another question, just out of curiosity."

"I'm listening."

"Is Ben's dad around? I've never heard him talk about him before and I was just wondering if you two were still together or if he grew up with him."

"His father left when he was very young, he probably doesn't talk about it because it causes him a lot of pain. Do me a favor and don't ask him anything else about him. If you really love Benjamin, respect his boundaries."

That line alone told me that there were some things about Benjamin's past that were hidden. However, I could see the look of irritation written across his mother's face so I quickly changed the subject. We started talking about the kids and the wedding and she seemed to get back to being comfortable with me. We continued talking throughout the whole day while Benjamin was out with his brothers that I hadn't even had a chance to meet yet. This time I could confirm that they actually were related to him since his mother spoke highly of all three of them.

She began cooking dinner while I went to the bathroom to go soak in the tub. I spent my alone time getting my thoughts together and finally mustering up the strength and courage to talk to God.

"Lord, I feel as though you have placed me in an impossible situation. For the sake of reliving it in my own mind, I won't go over the details but please Lord, fix this. I can't go through the pain and heartache that I've been through before so please Lord, I'm asking you to fix this."

That prayer did a lot of good for me, I wish I could have gotten it out before when I first found out about Ben but I was glad it came out at all. Sometimes all it takes is a few minutes alone with The Lord to get you back to where you need to be.

After that bath, I felt refreshed in my body and renewed in my spirit. I walked out just in time to meet all of Ben's brothers too. Ben was the youngest, then there was James, Joseph, and Daniel. I could tell by their names that their momma was instilled in the word of the Lord. They were all very handsome with their own unique looks and personalities, yet similar enough to tell they were brothers. They all seemed to like me a lot and treated me just as well as their mom did. The only time things got a bit strange was when I asked them if they had wives, they all said no. Three boys, four if you include Ben, and none of them were married. They all claimed that they were more focused on their careers and I guess that did make practical sense but something in my soul didn't fully believe what they were telling me. I didn't lament on it though, I figured whatever I was intuitively feeling about them would eventually reveal itself. During dinner time, we all sat around a big family table. Ben's momma was very big on family which was something I could appreciate since it reminded me of my momma. We all were exchanging stories about our childhoods and the different things that we went through. The boys talked about how they experienced some depression in their childhood and how they struggled financially. They talked about how they went through sleepless nights with little food and having to split one piece of steak between the four of them. Their story reminded me a lot of mine, albeit with its own unique differences. Like me they all started working at a young age, however they bought themselves out of poverty as a family compared to me taking on the financial responsibility after the death of my father. When I explained this to them, they lauded me and showed me plenty of compassion. They said my family was blessed to have a child like me, that anyone would be blessed to have me in their life. It made me feel good that someone felt that way about me because I didn't feel that way about my own self most of the time.

I started to become so comfortable talking to them that I had almost forgotten about what I had found out about Ben until he decided to skip dessert. His momma seemed surprised but his brother's all began looking at one another conspicuously, as if they knew where he was about to go. He gave me a quick kiss and left.

After he left, I wasn't in the mood for talking or continuing to sit there with Ben's family. I excused myself from the table after scarfing down the apple pie his momma had made and put all the kids to bed. I went to bed myself and before I could close my eyes, I heard a knock on the door. I told them they could come in and it ended up being Benjamin's oldest brother, Daniel. He wanted to sit down and talk to me and even though I really wasn't in the mood, I was curious as to what he had to say.

"You're a very beautiful girl, Deborah. My brother's a lucky man," he told me.

"Thank you Daniel, I appreciate you saying that. You know, you could always find yourself a good woman as well."

"I could but I'm not really interested in that."

"Yeah I know what you said, you're more focused on making a name for yourself doing whatever it is you do but that shouldn't deprive you of having a life."

"You're right, it shouldn't and it doesn't. I do have a life Deborah, just not the one that people think I should have."

"Well what kind of life do you have?"

"Well for one, inventing things is part of my life. That's what I like to do, create different toys for kids and sell them to companies. I make a good amount of money doing it too."

"Well Ben never told me that, that's very unique. I don't think I've ever met a person who could do something like that. But don't you ever want time to love someone? To be held? To take a drive out to the country and just enjoy yourself? Don't you want that with somebody?"

"I do have it with someone," he said.

"You do? Well then I apologize, I didn't realize you already have a woman in your life. Well come on, tell me what the lucky lady's name is." He paused for a minute then said,

"It isn't a woman Deborah, it's a man. And his name is Mario, he's my boyfriend."

It made sense, he didn't have a wife and no interest in one at all so I knew somewhere deep down inside that he was queer. "You mean, you're queer?" He nodded. "Well, does your family know about your boyfriend? Does anyone know besides me?"

"My brothers know."

"Even Ben?" I asked.

"Yes, he knows too."

"You know, people get beat for that kind of stuff, Daniel. You could get in real trouble, even with the law if the wrong person saw you kissing another man in public. I just heard a few days ago about some riots going on between queers and the authorities. A lot of people got hurt and everything. You don't want to be one of those people, do you?" I didn't know it at that time, but what I said probably hurt him a lot deeper than what he expressed. I had made him feel guilty for just being attracted to someone. I was very ignorant at that time and wish I had dealt with the situation in a lot better fashion. But I was young, I didn't know or understand what he had just told me. Luckily, he didn't hold it against me. He simply told me,

"I understand what you're saying Deborah and I believe you're coming from a loving place. If I'm being honest with you, I'm not the only one in my family like this. My brothers are as well, although if they knew I told you, they'd beat me 'til I passed out."

"Then why are you telling me?" I asked.

"Because you seem like a very sweet girl, very young and have a lot going for yourself. I don't want you to waste your time on anyone who isn't going to be as interested in you as you are in them. I want you to experience a life of happiness, nothing less." After he said that, he kissed me on the forehead and left the room. I was left speechless, I was just told by my soon-to-be brother-in-law that I should leave Ben. Sure he didn't say it directly but I knew exactly what he was trying to say. Daniel cared about me enough to be honest with me, but instead of taking his warning seriously, I ignored it and stayed with Benjamin. I could have left in that moment and everything in my life what have been completely different, but I didn't leave. I stayed.

I stayed with a man that I knew would never love me for who I really was.

CHAPTER SIX

After the wedding, we had decided that it was time for us to move to a new home. We got married in June, and that following December I gave birth to a baby boy and named him Norman James. He was beautiful and light skinned, just like his father. I loved him to pieces from the moment I first held him. The Lord was so gracious in how He'd continued to bless me with such a huge family, nothing ever convinced me otherwise. Ben loved the kids equally as well as I did. He always made it a goal to treat them the same way he was treated growing up, with love, respect, and a unity of family. As much as I hate to say it, he was in some ways better to the kids than I was. I loved being a mother, truly I did, but I think that years of dealing with Ben's affairs and my choosing to stay with him spilled over into how I treated my children. God bless all of them for what they had to endure because of the decisions I made and how I felt about my life. They didn't ask to be in this world nor to be victims of my pain I hadn't dealt with. I tried so hard not to take my anger out on my kids, but I felt like I was in a situation that I didn't know how to escape or make better. Sin and bondage has its grip on me, but I believed that God would eventually somehow deliver me and my kids from the trauma we suffered through. This was the prayer I constantly held for my children every night before I went to bed. I just wanted them...and myself, to be free.

Before we left Alabama for good and moved on to Pensacola, I decided I needed to close a few doors. I had my eldest son watch over his siblings and make sure things didn't get out of hand while I took a long drive by myself. The first place I visited was my momma's house of course. She was living by herself at that point and I just wanted to let her know much I really loved her before I left. When I went over there she was cooking some food for herself and seemed to be in the same serious mood I had always seen her in growing up. When I told her that Ben, the kids, and I were leaving town she didn't seem too affected by it. All she said to me was,

"Well Debbie, ever since you built this new life with Ben, it's been one change after another. All I can say is stay in prayer at all times and may The Lord be with you." I told her thank you and not long after that, I left. It was strange, my momma was so disconnected now. I mean she had never been one to show much emotion but she really seemed docile, almost as if she didn't care that I was leaving or what was going on in my life. Sad to say, I didn't pay too much attention to how she reacted because I knew how much she disapproved of Ben. Like I told her before, Ben was a good man. Yes, he had many faults but I loved him and that's all that mattered to me.

After leaving her house I decided to stop by my daddy's graveyard and say my goodbyes to him. It was one of the hardest goodbyes of my entire life. My daddy had been gone a long time at that point but it didn't change how much I loved him and missed him. If he had been alive at that time, so many other things in my life would have been different, but I digress. During my time of talking to him, hoping he could somehow hear me from Heaven, I let him know where I was going and everything that had happened in my life since he died. I told him about Ben, of course, and Papa Joe, even though I know they were already in Heaven partying together and watching over me. Then I told him about Mr. Ben, that was the hardest thing to talk about but I'm glad I did it. If I hadn't done it then I wouldn't have been led to go to Mr. Ben's house after I left the graveyard. I remember how long the drive was there, I had never noticed it before. It seemed like it took darn near half a day to get to his house but I can contribute that to how nervous I felt about going. I knew it was potentially dangerous and it

could result in me having a gun pulled out
on me either by Mr. Ben himself or his wife.
But I had to take the risk, I had to close the
most important chapter of my life in
Alabama.

When I got there, I rang the doorbell and
initially no one answered. I took a look
around and noticed how he had remodeled
the entire farm. I can tell business had been
booming which I guess made sense since he
was put in charge after Papa Joe died. After
a few doorbell rings, and almost deciding
that I had made a mistake in going, I heard
footsteps approach the door. My heart began
to race the same way it always used to when

I was about to see him or be around him in general. The door opened slowly and there he was, Mr. Ben stared me right in the face. He studied me for a few seconds, I guess because I had looked so different since the last time he'd seen me. I was a full grown adult now and my body had really started to fill out the way it was meant to. After looking shocked and speechless for a few minutes, he said,

"Deborah, is that you?"

"Yes, it is. I wanted to come see you." He paused then made that same big grin he used to back when I worked for him.

"Come in, please," he said. As I walked in, I noticed how different the place looked. It wasn't as clean as it used to be when I worked for him, and it had an odor to it that reminded me of teenagers, which made sense since his kids were older now. He noticed my observing and tried to defend himself.

"Sorry about the place, I know it isn't clean like it used to be."

"I'm not judging Mr. Ben, I'm just glad you let me in," I told him.

"Why wouldn't I? You did used to practically run this place."

"Oh now I wouldn't go that far Mr. Ben, I was just a servant."

"You were more than a servant Deborah, you were like a mother to my children and a wife to me." When he said that I blushed like I was a teenage girl all over again. It amazed me that after all these years, he still had his way with words when it came to me. But I had to be careful, I knew I was a married woman and did not want to cheat even if my husband was doing so. "Why don't I get you something to drink?" he offered.

"I can get it, I remember where fridge is." He insisted on getting it himself and I let him, there was no need to be rude or disrespectful in someone else's house.

"You were always so independent Deborah, one of the many things I loved about you."

"Thank You for saying that, you know it's how I was raised."

"I remember, in fact I remember everything." I was beginning to get nervous when he said that, it felt like he was trying to keep open doors that I had come there to close. I decided it would be best if we just diverted the subject of the past.

"Where's your wife?" I asked.

He replied sharply, "She doesn't stay here anymore."

"What? Why, what happened?"

"One day I walked in from handling some business out of town and found out she was having an affair with that old racist bastard, Evan. I'm sure you remember him."

"I do remember him."

"Yeah well he and my wife are married now. He took her and the kids and ran off. Left me with nothing." I couldn't believe what he just said, his wife ran off with another man and Mr. Evan of all people. I remember seeing the look of pain in his eyes when he told me about it and I couldn't help but comfort him. It was all innocent and out of love, I had no intention of doing anything except comforting my friend and old boss. I was holding him for some time, just so he knew how much I cared about him. But somehow in my attempt to show my friendship, a message was misinterpreted.

"Deborah, I'm sorry for kicking you out the way I did. I'm sorry for treating you the way I did. I was so upset about you being with Joseph that I just wanted to get back at you. I wanted you to feel what I felt but I should have just forgiven you. Just like how you had to forgive me for being with my wife when I should have been with you."

"Now Mr. Ben that's old news, everything happens for a reason. I'm happy with my life now and I'm sure you'll be happy with yours too once you find someone nice for you."

"I can be happy again, Deborah, if you come back to me."

"Mr. Ben I appreciate it but I'm married now, I have a family," I told him. He stopped crying, pulled away from me, and stared at me. I expected him to snap at me. It was the same stare that he gave me when he raised his hand to hit me, except this time Papa Joe wasn't there to protect me.

"I think I should go Mr. Ben" He saw the look of fear in my eyes as I tried to get up and leave. He followed me and pulled me towards him.

"Don't leave me Deborah, I'm sorry. I shouldn't have raised my hand to hit you the way I did last time, I shouldn't have scared you. I should have just loved you."

"Mr. Ben like I said, all that's in the past. I moved on and I really should get—"

"Shhhhh." He pulled me closer and whispered "make love to me Deborah, let's make love like we used to." I tried to tell him no, that I was married and not interested. I tried fighting him off, but it was no use. He was determined and I was weak. Not just physically, but emotionally.

I gave in and did it, I made love to Mr. Ben right there on the same sofa in his living room that I sat on when he raised his hand at me.

When we were finished, I couldn't believe what I had done. I hadn't even been married to Ben a month and already I had

cheated on him. I felt low, worthless. I knew

I had to get back home and be with

Benjamin again before things got even

worse with Mr. Ben. I told him I had to go,

but he wasn't willing to let me so easily.

"Deborah, it's been so long since

we've laid down with one another like this.

Making love to you was even better than

how I remember. Don't be in a rush, I

understand you have a home to go back to.

But before you go, before you leave me, just

give me a few more minutes. Please." He

didn't understand, I wasn't in a rush to get

back to Benjamin. Yes, I loved him with

everything in me but I knew what true love

was. As guilty and dishonorable as I felt after cheating on him with Mr. Ben, I still knew deep down that the way I felt about Mr. Ben would never go away.

After a few hours well into the night, I finally got ready to leave. I had avoided telling Mr. Ben the whole time that I was getting ready to move. It was partially on purpose but I also got caught up in our time together. Reminiscing, wanting my life to go back to the way it used to be. But I knew in my spirit that that time in my life was over, the story of me and Mr. Ben had already been written. He didn't need to know about the child I kept from him that I believe to be his and not Papa Joe's, he didn't need to know that a part of me wanted to drop Benjamin and start a life with him, he didn't need to know a lot of things that ran through my mind. I shared enough with him, I shared my body and a whole part of my life with him. So after I told him I was moving, I kissed him goodbye and left for good. But what I'll never forget is how hard I cried on the ride home, I knew in that moment that Mr. Ben was my true soulmate.

When I got back home, I expected Benjamin to be either at work or out doing whatever it is he used to do when he wasn't around me. Probably with some man, some man that could never give him the love or the child I gave him. But I had no room to be bitter or hard-hearted after what I had done. I walked into the house and had my intentions of just going to bed. But when I got to my bedroom, I noticed the door was locked. I thought maybe one of the kids had locked themselves in there so I knocked as hard as I could. I didn't get an answer. I remember being so tired and had enough on my mind to where my patience was running low, and I just wanted to lie down. The bedroom had a window from the outside that you could use to enter in case of emergencies, almost similar to a door. I went outside and walked around to enter it that way. But when I got to the window I saw Benjamin lying on his back butt-naked and no sheet over him.

I wasn't suspicious that anything was going on, just figured that maybe he was just tired from a long day. Then I saw a man walking from the bathroom area and into the bed, the bed we shared together. They began lying down, kissing one and holding each other. I wanted to bust through that window and kill them, but I held my temper. I thought about getting in my car and going back to Mr. Ben's house and spending the rest of the night with him. I thought about just leaving but I got this feeling. What if one of the kids woke up and went to the bedroom? Either they would end up seeing Benjamin in bed with another man from going through the outside window, or they might just stay outside the door and cry. I didn't want that happening, I loved my kids with all my heart.

So, I got out the car and headed inside and to the couch to lie down. I figured I would just let Benjamin have his privacy for the night while I stayed and kept a lookout for the kids in case they woke up. By the grace of God they never did, and when morning came, I woke up to the smell of Benjamin cooking breakfast. Eggs, bacon, grits, all of my favorites. I didn't know if he was doing it out of guilt or love but I didn't care, I was just happy that the night was over and that it was now morning. I walked to the kitchen to help Ben out with the cooking but much to my surprise, there was a man, the same man from last night, helping him cook.

"Good morning!" I said. I must have startled the both of them because they almost jumped out of their skin when they heard me.

"Debbie, you're awake?" Ben asked.

"Yes, you didn't think I'd sleep the day away on the couch did you?" I told him.

"No, of course not. Sorry about the bedroom being locked last night, my cousin was asleep and I didn't want to wake him up." That excuse again, his cousin. Of course he knew that I knew it wasn't his cousin but I decided to play a long for a little while. But I wanted so badly to call him out on this supposed cousin however I didn't want to start a fight with the kids in the house.

"Oh okay, it wasn't a problem. Why don't you introduce us?" I told him.

"Of course," he said. "Eddie this is my beautiful wife Deborah and Deborah this one of my favorite cousins, Eddie."

"Nice to meet you Eddie"

"You too," he replied as he gave me a false smile. I didn't want to be too antagonistic with him but after what I saw last night, I deserved some answers.

"So Eddie, are you from around here? Only reason I ask is cause Ben always tells me that his family is all down in Florida, I wasn't even aware that he had a cousin here." After I said that, Eddie looked like he just saw a ghost. He was trying to think of a lie quick but I could tell he wasn't used to dealing with a smart southern woman. Ben interceded.

"He isn't from here, he actually just moved here from a town right outside of Pensacola named Destin."

"Oh okay, well have you told him that we're moving down to Pensacola?" I asked. Eddie became red, you could tell that he was holding in some anger and confusion. It was my guess that he and Ben had probably been messing with each other for a while at that point because he seemed like he was a little hurt.

"No, he didn't tell me actually. Didn't hear anything about it until now," he said in an embittered tone.

"I was actually going to tell him today but you just spoiled the surprise." He made a glance at me like he wanted to choke the life out of me like he almost did the first time.

"I apologize. Why don't I let you two talk and I'll go wake the kids up for breakfast?" I told him.

"Good idea," Benjamin said as he gave me an evil glare. I went to wake the kids as I said I would and while I was doing so, I could hear them arguing but trying to keep their voices down. I guess I must have caused something between him and his boyfriend (or whatever he was) but I felt no remorse. He was married to me after all and had no business cheating. Of course, who was I to even think that, I couldn't forget about what I had done with Mr. Ben, but I felt justified in that. I wasn't of course, but at that time I wanted a way to make my own self feel better in my supposed self-righteous.

After I got the kids awake and washed up for breakfast, we all went to the kitchen. The table was already set for me and the kids but Benjamin and his "boyfriend" were gone. I almost cried, but what was the point? I knew by then the marriage and the life I had signed up for, so I got the kids and we all ate breakfast together like we were supposed to. After we were done, I had spent some time with Norman until he fell back to sleep and then began packing the house up so we could get ready to leave.

It was in those moments that I found what I consider to be some of my greatest peace. Even though my hands were busy, my mind was completely at peace. Despite all the things I had been through, I could only think of all the possibilities that could come with being in a new place. I had been through so much in Alabama and to finally have a chance to leave all of that behind was like a death and rebirth for me. I may not have had a perfect marriage, but I did have the chance to start something completely new. I had a chance to leave behind the place where I had gotten heartbroken on multiple occasions, been fired from a job for something that wasn't even my fault, and lost my father and even Papa Joe. I was just so ready and eager to leave everything behind so I could finally begin writing my own story from scratch.

Later on that night, Ben came home. By the time he had gotten there, the kids were in bed and I had just about everything in the house packed. We weren't supposed to leave 'til the next day at around noon time, but I was accustomed to getting things done early. When he got there, I could tell he wasn't feeling too good. He slammed the front door as he walked in and started aggressively moving boxes out of his way. I went up to him to ask him what was wrong and he ignored me. He walked back towards the bedroom and slammed the door. My heart was beating with all the fear I felt every time situations like that arose. I knew deep down that something was about to happen though I wasn't sure what exactly it was. I went to the bedroom door and tried to open it, it was locked. I knocked "Ben, can you let me in? If you aren't feeling well then we can always talk, just please let me in." I stayed there knocking and begging for five minutes until he came to the door with bloodshot eyes and stared at me. "What the hell do you want, Deborah?"

"I just want to make sure you're okay, that's what a good wife does isn't it?"

He looked annoyed. I think he knew I wasn't just trying to comfort him, I was also teasing him. A part of me knew—or at least hoped–that some of his negativity came from his boyfriend breaking up with him. With that in mind, I walked in the room with the intention of giving myself to him. I figured if nothing else, at least sex would make him feel better since he obviously had such a big fascination for it. But as I tried to seduce him, he slapped my hand away and told me,

"I don't want to have sex with you Deborah, get the hell away from me."

"Why?" I asked. "I'm your wife and I just want to lift up your spirits. Nothing lifts up a man like the body of a woman, right?" He looked at me disgusted by my attempts to make him feel better mixed with my teasing.

"Deborah, you're a piece of work. You think I don't know what you were trying to do this morning? How you were trying to piss me off by humiliating me in front of Eddie?" His anger was intensifying, and I knew at that point that my teasing had gotten me into a bad situation.

"What are you talking about Ben? I really was just trying to inform him that we were leaving. Since he was your cousin, I didn't think you'd mind me telling him"

"Deborah, I'm not stupid. You think that I'm blind to the fact that my brother talked to you when we were in Florida? Or that you have been spying on me every time I bring a man around? I know about everything you've been doing, even right down to who you went to see last night."

He caught me off guard, I didn't expect what he had told me. If Benjamin knew I was on to him and what he was doing and even worse, if he was on to me and what I did with Mr. Ben, then that meant he had been playing me all along. I kept thinking that I had somehow married someone who was even sicker than I was. "You want to play games Deborah? You want to try to be an independent woman who shames and divorces her husband? I'm not letting it happen, I guarantee that." His tone was dark, it didn't feel so much like a game anymore. The man I had made an oath to was scaring me, I didn't know whether I wanted to hit him and run in that minute or jump his bones and make love to him. It sounds sadistic but it was part of the effect that Ben and all the unhealthy relationships I had in the past had on me. He looked at me like a demon was inside of him.

I felt the urge to grab the bottle that was on the dresser next to the bed but before I could get to it, he backhanded me in the face. I fell down to the bed and he got on top of me and began choking me. As I was running out of breath, he whispered in my ear, "I need to make sure you never feel the need to cheat on me again. You are my wife and you belong to me, no one else." He then let go his grip on me and for a minute I was relieved until he started ripping my clothes off and forcing himself in me. I wanted scream but I knew it was no use, who would hear me? Who could save me? The only other people in the house or anywhere near us was my children and I didn't want them to see what their dad was doing to me. So, as I had become accustomed to so many times in my life, I didn't fight it. I gave in and figured that it was easier and better than fighting back, at least then I would keep the peace.

Peace, that's what I told myself. But it was

but it was anything but peace.

CHAPTER SEVEN

A few years later, around 1966, my life with Benjamin was well established. I gave birth to my 15th child, Rose. She was my pride and joy; I didn't like to pick favorites but boy did I love her. From the time she was first born, I knew I had given birth to a special child. Ben loved her too, even more so than the other kids. He would always spend father-daughter days with her and spoil her, much like how my father and I were. I guess watching their relationship helped make my marriage to Ben all the more tolerable. From our time of moving to Florida, things didn't get better in our marriage, but they did balance out. I had started to become used to him leaving the house and sleeping with different men and women, having children outside our marriage, doing whatever he wanted to do. A small part of me had convinced myself that this was the life I always dreamed of, after all, Ben didn't leave me or die. He always stayed with me no matter what we went through. No matter how many words we used to attack one another or how many times he came home and hit me or forced himself on me when I wasn't willingly giving it up. It was a life that I could handle, I had kids and I had a husband. Back in those times, that was considered to be a major part of the American dream. And it helped that we weren't hurting for money since I had the inheritance from Papa Joe's passing and Ben was constantly securing odd jobs from fixing cars to building things and selling them, all types of entrepreneurship. People on the outside, such as our neighbors, envied our relationship. They always looked at us as if we were the perfect well off couple. At that time I was in my mid 30's and thought it was cool to be the envy of people around me. It made me feel better about what the real truth was. That I was not in a perfect marriage, in fact it was far from perfect. But I will say that even with the trouble the marriage came with, I still consider myself more blessed than many. Not everyone had the blessing of being able to stay in a seven bedroom house and have everything already paid off. Along with that, I was also able to have plenty of time to help out neighbors, both financially and otherwise. I had neighbors who house I would go over just to cook for them and their families whenever their wives were at work or they were too busy trying to balance taking care of kids and maintaining a house. Given my history it came natural for me, plus I had instilled a strong spirit of independence in my children so it was never an issue to leave them at home with no supervision except each other. I took pride in how well my kids were behaved because they knew that if they had ever gotten out of line, I would quickly put them back in it. I did have some kids that were better behaved than others though, like any parent. My sixth child, Bennie, proved to be one of those kids who were a bit more difficult to handle. Most of my kids would argue that he was my favorite along with Rose, but what they didn't understand is that parents tend to treat their children based on the child's needs. I knew that Bennie required extra love and attention because he was always up to something. When he was a kid, his teachers would always end up giving him a beating at school for behaving inappropriately. He and

Benjamin used to clash because of this but I always made sure he didn't go too far with trying to discipline him. In fact I can only remember one time when I was upset enough with Benny to beat him at all. He had come home from school one day and said he had something to tell me.

"What did you do this time? If you keep on misbehaving, I'm gone beat your ass." It sounded like tough words but I had to present myself with some authority. Truth is I was only trying to intimidate him. That is until I found out what he needed to say.

"Momma I don't know how to tell you this but I got in trouble in school today."

"How much trouble? You weren't bullying someone again were you?"

"No ma'am"

"So what did you do, Benny?" It was almost impossible to get an answer out of him, he just kept staring at me and shaking. Then he lifted up his shirt and showed me where his teacher had beat him. It was more than just some regular spank on the behind, he had bruises across his whole body. At that point, I knew whatever he had done had to be serious so I looked at him and asked "Benny, what in the hell did you do?"

He replied, "I...I messed with a girl in the bathroom."

"You mean you were caught having sex in the bathroom? Boy I oughta beat your ass again! You know better than to do be doing something like that at school!" He looked at me with fear in his eyes, and seeing that on your child's face will do something to you no matter what they did. His look broke me down and made me hug him, I figured he had enough chastising as it was. There was no need for me to add on to his punishment. But I had the feeling that maybe he was still leaving something out, still not telling me the full story. I looked at him and asked him if I was right. He confirmed I was.

"There is more momma. Because of what I did, I was expelled from school." he told me. My blood ran cold, I didn't know how to react. I understood the seriousness of what he had done but for him to get expelled and be completely kicked out of the school seemed extreme. At that point I wasn't so much upset with him as I was with the situation and with the girl, without even knowing who she was. I kept thinking how she corrupted my son and how he had to pay the consequences for it.

"Well what about the girl? Did she get expelled too?" I asked.

"No, ma'am" he replied bluntly.

"Well why the hell not?" I asked. He looked at me like he was afraid to answer so I told him to come with me, that we were going to school together to solve the issue immediately.

When we got there, I demanded a meeting with the principal, Ms. Wiggins was her name. It wasn't very hard to get it being that she was one of the only staff members left at the school. As I walked into her office with my son behind me, she gave him an evil glare and I was about ready to take out all of the anger that had been building up in me over the years. But I remained humble. I knew that even though I believed my son, I should hear the full story from an adult. As we sat down in the office, we got straight to the conversation.

"I'm sure you know why I'm here today Ms. Wiggins?" I asked.

"Yes ma'am, I assume it's regarding your son and his inappropriate behavior—to say the least," she replied.

"That's part of the reason why. The other being why the girl he engaged in intercourse with didn't receive the same punishment as him. Last time I checked it takes two to tango if you understand what I'm saying,"

"I'm not sure I do understand, Mrs. James. There's no reason for your son's victim to get punished when he's the one who forced himself on her. That's hardly a reason to punish someone unless you are the type of person who approves of such things and if you are, then perhaps I need to call child protective services." I couldn't believe what she had just said. I needed to verify to make sure I heard her correctly.

"Excuse me, Ms. Wiggins, but are you saying that my son did not engage in consensual intercourse with the girl? That he...." I couldn't finish the words, I almost burst into tears. Partially out of humiliation, partially out of disbelief.

"Yes ma'am, that is correct. I'm assuming from your reaction that your son told you otherwise which doesn't surprise me being that he's a little degenerate." That was the wrong thing to say to a mother who had just found out her prized child was troubled, beyond troubled in fact. Without saying a word I reached over the table and grabbed her by her throat.

"Listen here, bitch, if you ever in your life say anything like that about any of my children again then I will personally slit your damn throat. Do you understand me, nigga?" She nodded her head and looked at me with so much fear that I was even afraid of myself. I threw her down on the floor, releasing my grip on her. After that I grabbed my son and got the hell out of there.

When we got in the car, I was silent during the whole ride home. He knew better than to say anything to me, my first impulse was to pull over on the side of the road and beat him until he turned black and blue. But I knew that wouldn't help, no he needed to be dealt with by his father. Benjamin never liked disciplining, and they hated when he did it versus me because the few times he did it, he took it too far. Truth is I couldn't do it, I was afraid I'd kill the damn boy. Bad behavior is one thing but to force yourself on someone at school? Did I give birth to the devil or something? In those moments, I hate to say it but I regretted ever becoming a mother. How did I raise a child that turned out to be so evil and troublesome? I knew he was mischievous of course, but that was nothing compared to what he had done to that poor girl. I had men force themselves on me plenty of times and although I didn't fight back, I can't imagine another person being in that position and especially at such a young age. Benny had to learn that what he did was the worst kind of thing you could do to a person so when we got home, I took him right to Benjamin.

"Ben, our son has something to tell you," I told him.

"Okay. What is it?" Benny didn't say anything, he just looked at me like a lost puppy hoping I would spare him from having to confess his sins to his father. "Benny, what do you have to tell me? No matter how bad you think it is, talk to me." Benny stood behind me, he was not going to say anything and my patience was running thin.

"Dammit boy if you won't tell him, I will. Our son was expelled from school today." I told him.

"Expelled? For what? What did he do?"

"He thought it was okay to force himself on one of his classmates in the bathroom. The young girl was—" Before I could finish, Benjamin cut me off.

"You forced yourself on a young girl in the bathroom?" Benny nodded, still trying to hold on to me. Ben continued. "I see. Debbie excuse me for a minute, I'm going to talk to our son alone."

"Well I sure as hell hope you gon' do more than just talk to him, you need to discipline him Ben. He needs to know that this kind of behavior isn't acceptable for anyone!"

"Debbie, I will handle it. I don't need help in what to say to my son, now excuse yourself from the room before I have to remove you myself." There it was, me once again being talked to like a slave, like I was less than. But because there was a more important matter at hand to handle, I didn't argue with him and did as asked. I don't know what Benjamin said to him that day but I didn't hear a scream nor a cry of any kind. In fact, Benny only grow even more out of control after that day.

About a year later, I found myself pregnant yet again. It was my final child and I named him Damon. At that point Ben and I had sixteen kids overall, including the kids I had with Papa Joe and Mr. Ben. I'd told Ben that I'd rather get my uterus taken out then have any more kids, it was nothing against him but I had a big enough family. It didn't help that I felt as if my parenting skills were decreasing and my frustration was increasing. It seemed like whenever I tried to do something positive, there was always a force working against me. For example, we were able to get Benny enrolled in school again and he even placed high enough on a test to skip the eighth grade and go straight to high school. But, we were having trouble out of one of our other boys, Gabriel. He was about fifteen years old at that time and was very smart and handsome, much like Benjamin. But he could never seem to stay away from the streets or local gang violence. Ben and I tried everything we could just to get him straight and make sure he stayed on the right path in life. But he was stubborn, he wanted things his way and no one else's way. He did not heed instruction from either his mother or his father and as a result, we lost him. Boy I still remember that day and how much it pained me to lose one of my children. Gabriel was going up to the gas station not too far from the house on a hot Saturday afternoon. He had come back within half an hour but he was all fired up from some altercation he had been involved in. Ben and I tried to get him to calm down but he was persistent in his anger. He walked out the house with a gun in his hand and said he was going to make the people who had pissed him off regret whatever they said to him. We both tried so hard to stop him but he pushed us out the way and told us to stay out of his way. A few hours later, we had gotten a call from the authorities asking us if we was Gabriel's parents. I told him yes and he told me Gabriel had gotten shot and had passed away. I dropped the phone and fell to my knees shouting to God "why!" Ben tried to comfort me but he was in no state to do so himself; he and Gabriel were so close. I tell you it doesn't matter how many children a mother and father has, the pain of losing even one of them is something that can never be replaced. We tried praying the pain away, drinking it away, we even tried screwing it away in the bedroom. None of it worked, none of the pain we experienced ever went away. We just had to learn to face this new reality that we had, we had to learn to deal with our situation in whatever way we possibly could. That day both Ben and I had a change for the worse. They say that death brings people closer together, but for us, it only pulled us even further apart.

As a time went by, the kids and I would do whatever we could to try to be closer with one another. Ben kept working, even more than usual. I knew that he wasn't just working though, I knew he was spending time with one of these women he used to have come over. He didn't even try to say that she was his cousin or anything, he said she was a friend and at that point I could really care less. I had begun seeing a man myself on the side named Tony, or Mr. T as I liked to call him. Like Ben, he was a lighter skin man and very attractive, but unlike Ben, he was nice, always treated me with respect. "When are you gonna leave that husband of yours?" He always used to ask. "When The Lord Jesus tells me to," I would tell him. I had no intentions of leaving Benjamin, we had a full family to take care of. Of course by that point my first few kids were all gone off to live their own lives and everything but I still wanted the rest of my kids to grow up with a full family unit. Ben didn't too much care for family though at that point, his actions showed it.

Our son Norman had told me one day that he needed to have a talk with me about Ben. I always tried to be open with my kids and let them know that they could come to me about absolutely anything in the world. Norman sat down with me said, "Momma, daddy's been doing something for a long time that I'm not sure you know about." Now I figured that he had somehow found out about his father messing around with different women and was somehow about to burst my bubble, in his mind anyway. But, I didn't want to jump to conclusions so I humored him.

"Your dad usually tells me about everything he does. A man doesn't hide secrets from his wife," I told him.

"Well this is a secret he kept for a reason momma. He knows you would lose it if you found out." At that point, I knew that he knew about the cheating so I came clean.

"Listen Norman, you're almost an adult now and you know enough for me to tell you this. I know about what your father does with other women but I stay with him anyway because I love him. Now it may not be what some people think of as love, but it is love in its own way, son, I promise you.

One day you'll understand." I was hoping my confession would stop the conversation but Norman looked at me with a look a mother never wants to see her child give her. He said,

"It's not that mom, this has nothing to do with dad cheating. This is about how he—" before he could finish, we heard Benjamin waking up and walking out of the bedroom. He came to the door and shouted for me to meet him in the room which usually meant he wanted some. I wasn't too eager about giving it up to him but he was my husband so I had an obligation.

"Why don't we finish this later, okay honey?" I said to him. As I got up and tried to walk away, Norman shouted at the top of his lungs,

"Mom wait! Don't go in there with daddy, he's a rapist. He raped me momma, dad raped me!" I stopped dead in my tracks and it seemed like the household grew dead silent. On top of everything else I had known about Ben, I had never known him to touch any of our kids. That was something he just wouldn't do, even in his perversions he always loved our children. I turned around and looked at Norman who was on the floor crying like a little kid after what he had just told me. Before I could even head towards him to comfort him or confirm what he said, Ben came storming out of the bedroom with a belt. He pushed me out of the way and went straight for Norman. He tried to run but it was no use, Ben was in great shape and could move like a racehorse.

He grabbed Norman by the back of the shirt and shouted, "What have I told you about running your mouth telling lies! Now I'm gonna beat the lies out of you devil child!" He began beating him so hard I think the good Lord Himself had to turn away so He wouldn't have to look at what was happening. I stood there in shock, listening to my son's ear-piercing screams shout my name, begging for help. I didn't help him, I didn't know how to help him. I had no time to discern the situation to see if it was true and quite frankly Ben's anger had me too terrified to even move. After about ten minutes of him beating Norman, Benjamin told him to get out of his face and go wash up so he could make dinner. He then walked past me and demanded me to meet him in the bedroom. I was afraid not to, afraid to disobey him. I'd seen Ben angry before but this was different, it was like a spirit came over him and amplified whatever he was feeling on the inside. As I followed him into the bedroom, he slammed the door shut and looked me in the eyes.

"You don't believe that shit he was saying, do you?" he asked.

"No...no, Ben, I don't believe him. I know you, and you love our kids, you wouldn't do anything like that."

"Good answer." "But it still doesn't change anything." he continued.

"What are you talking about?"

"I'm talking about how you still stood there and listened to him. When I call you, you are to come immediately. But since you wanted to let your curiosity get the best of you, you're about to reap the shit seeds that you sowed." I started backing away from him but it was too late. He took the belt and slapped me across my face. I felt blood trickle down my face on to my chest. He then punched me in the face repeatedly and grabbed me by the throat. Slammed me down on the floor and ripped my clothes off. He started whipping me again and again and again with the belt until I had marks all over my body. I begged him to stop and every time I spoke, he hit a little bit harder. Then he stopped after what I swear was half an hour of just beating me half to death. He laid down on the bed and took his clothes off. Told me to get on top of him like I was riding a horse, that if I refused then he would beat me again. I did as he asked, face soaked in tears and body covered with bruises and blood. But I did it, I was obedient to my husband and did as he asked until he finished.

He kissed me afterwards and told me I should go take a shower so he could change the bed. When I went into that shower that night, I didn't just step into a tub with bruises all over me. I stepped into a baptism that would cleanse me of everything I had been through. Yes, I was getting baptized and was ready for my death and my subsequent resurrection.

CHAPTER EIGHT

That night I had experienced had stuck with me, it determined all of my actions going forward. Years down the road, when my two youngest were in high school and the rest of the kids were long gone living their own lives, I had begun to plan my escape. There was no reason to stay with a husband that had no respect for me, no desire for me in any form, he just wanted control over me. The years following that terrible night were horrible on our marriage and family. My kids had grown apart from me and wanted little to do with Ben. Ben and I would constantly get into fights, and I began fighting him back. I had gotten to the point where I really didn't care anymore. I started coming in the house, finding reasons to argue just like he did. Then I would take something in the house and bash him across the head with it. He would get me back later by waking me up out of my sleep with a switch or a belt. We constantly were at one another's throats, we lived in hell together. I felt bad that Rose and Damon didn't get to see what it was like to see their parents' have even a remotely good marriage. We didn't try to fake our relationship in front of them. How could we, we hated one another too much. I guess it stands to ask then why in the hell did we even bother staying together? Truth is, we were addicted to the pain. Every time after we argued or fought, we had sex. It wasn't the kind of love making that I had with Mr. Ben or even what I had with Papa Joe, no it was a power play. Sometimes it ended in him winning and sometimes it ended in me winning and forcing myself on him. I began bringing different men over and sleeping with them while he was at work. Sometimes he walked in while they were still there but I warned him not to say anything. That if he did, I would divorce him and take every penny of my inheritance and his money and leave him with nothing. I had to be tolerant of his male and female companions for years so he owed it to me to not say a damn word about what I was doing. I remember one day he came in and told me we needed to have a talk. "Okay, what do you want to talk about Ben"? I asked in the most sarcastic tone possible.

"What we've been doing to each other Debbie, it's wrong. We need to stop this, we need to fix our marriage," he pleaded. I laughed in his face and told him,

"We don't have a marriage Benjamin. There's nothing to fix."

"Debbie, I know I'm partly responsible for the way you are now. I made you become resentful and aggressive, I want to make it up to you. I want to go back to what we had decades ago," he told me.

"What we had decades ago? You mean lies and deceit? You going out and cheating on me and me somehow convincing myself that I'm okay with it? No Benjamin, I'd rather take what we have now. At least I can get some dick on the side the same way you do," I told him.

"Look Deb, I know you're upset about a lot of things I put you through, but I'm trying to make up for it now. I'm going to show you, Deborah, that I mean it, I want to be a better husband to you," he finished. He kissed me on the forehead after that and went to the bedroom leaving me speechless.

After what he said, I just wanted to burst into tears. Did he mean it? Was he really ready to give our marriage the makeover it needed, better yet was it even possible to start over? I would soon find out that it was, that starting over requires one thing—effort.

During the following months after our talk, things began to slowly change. Ben would spend more time at the house and try to spend time with Damon and Rose. He stopped seeing all his outside relationships and started preparing romantic dinners for me. I wasn't as gullible as he hoped I would be, a part of me felt like he had some hidden agenda behind it. Truth be told I was also beginning to really fall for Mr.T as well, so I wasn't going to just break off that relationship for a failed marriage. But as more time went on, he stayed consistent. He bought a new house for us, a three bedroom house with a built-in front porch and a summer house for my plants. He started changing up our love life, asking me if I was in the mood and complimenting me on my looks. It was like the Ben I had imagined when we first got together was finally beginning to manifest himself. He managed to do something I didn't even think was possible, got our kids to start back visiting. They brought their kids and for the first time, I had a chance to see my grandkids.

That brought me more joy than anything, being a grandmother. I think that was the turning point for me spiritually, I asked him if he was willing to go to church one Sunday and, surprisingly, he was. We had a good time and I think The Lord's favor was truly smiling down upon us because from the moment we walked in that church, people gravitated towards us. People we didn't know came up to us and told us how special our relationship was and that God had really blessed us. There was a part of me that thought they were half crazy 'cause if they knew what we had been through, I doubt blessed would be the right adjective. But I accepted their words and compliments. Who was I to reject a blessing of any kind after all?

After about a year of our renewed relationship, we decided it was appropriate to renew our wedding vows. I was so excited I went out and bought one of the most beautiful dresses in the world. I wanted to look like a queen because that was what I had felt like. After feeling low for so long, Ben had finally made me feel the way I hadn't felt since the beginning of our relationship.

We didn't have many friends so we had Rose and Damon as our maid of honor and best man, respectively. Just about all of our kids attended the wedding (except the one we lost, of course, and one of our daughters who had ceased contact with the family.) She never explained why she was so distant, only told Norman that she had no interest in talking to any of us and that she refused to tell anyone where she was. It broke my heart to hear that but I wanted to focus on the positive. I was getting ready to remarry a man that I hadn't been sure still existed, a man I wasn't sure ever existed. I remember the wedding vows I wrote for him that day, they were even more special than the ones from our first wedding.

"Benjamin James, you are the one man in this world that I can say understands the parts of me that no one else can see. You have been patient with me, we've been understanding with one another, and despite our problems, love has overcome everything we faced. So as I stand before you today, I proclaim my love to you just like I did decades ago, except I know you better now. And because I know you better, I can honestly say that I love you." He cried that day, I cried as I was saying it. I was never one to express myself too heavily to a person but I felt so much joy in being able to really start things fresh with him. When you've had a marriage like the one me and

Benjamin had, you look forward to moments when peace seems to take over.

Peace stayed with us for about three years following that day. But it was after those three years that we began to face trials again, ones that we would not be able to overcome like we had done before.

It started with our daughter, Rose. It was her senior year of high school and she came to us and told she was pregnant. At first we didn't mind, didn't really make a big deal out of it since I myself had a child during my teenage years. Honestly I was glad that at least she was pregnant during her last year of school, instead of being a high school dropout like me and end up having a child and not being sure who the father was. But then she showed me that the apple truly does not fall far from the tree. She wasn't aware of who the father of her child was. I asked her how she did not know. She told me that it could be one out of two guys but she wasn't sure which one it was. That made Ben furious, he couldn't believe that our daughter, our precious Rose, was even sexually active at all. We felt partially responsible since she grew up seeing the corruption and hardships of our relationship, but we knew we couldn't change the past, all we could do is do better going forward.

Rose's pregnancy was only the beginning of the downfall for us. Past demons that we both swore we had exercised decided to take a visit and launch an attack on our marriage. A woman came around the house one day while Ben and I were snuggled on the sofa together watching some afternoon soaps. She claimed that she had two children and that Benjamin was the father of both of them. Told us that the kids were around the age of 3 and 5 and that she was tired of taking care of the kids alone, she needed some help and needed Ben to step up to the plate. My first impulse was to go grab my gun so I could shoot the shit out of her, but I knew the nature of my and Ben's relationship just a few years ago. I knew she was probably telling the truth and after a few hours of talking to her, Ben had admitted that the kids were most likely his. That he was not only messing around with the woman at that time, he had promised to love her. That left a bit of a hole in my heart but I had no room to be judgmental. I kept telling myself that I just wanted us to push forward no matter what. We were able to work out a deal where Ben helped her take care of the kids and they even would spend some time over our house. I initially wasn't okay with it, but after some time, I grew to love them as if they were my own. The kids were so young and I knew they didn't ask to be there. Plus, having them around me and Ben made me feel like we had another chance at being better parents since we had failed so miserably with our own children. Sure, it bothered me that their mother was about twenty years my junior and she'd like to come over to the house dressed all skimpy attempting to get Ben's attention—but I pushed through it all. I was not going to let anything get in the way of my renewed relationship with Benjamin, but once again I failed to realize that some things are just simply too far out of my control.

After about a year of that incident, we had gotten a visit from Norman. It was good to see him, being that he didn't come around very often since he had such a complicated relationship with Ben. We updated him on his new half siblings and also told him about Rose's child that we had been helping her take care of. He wasn't too surprised to find out his sister had a baby, said with her beauty men had practically flocked towards her. I didn't disagree with him as I knew my daughter was a gem to be cherished. He told me he needed to talk to me alone one day and I was filled with anxiety since the last time he said that spurred a chain of traumatic events. He started asking me questions about his birth and asked me if Ben was his real father. I don't know what in the world made him even ask a question like that but I tried to assure him that Benjamin was his dad. No matter how he felt about him that was the only father he'd ever known and he had no reason to question it. He then told me he had visited my hometown in Alabama and ran into an older man with the same name as his father.

It was Mr. Ben. I had no clue how he ran into him but I was determined to deter that conversation as quickly as possible. Problem was Norman wasn't no fool; he was as sharp and observant as they came. He told me that he had decided to visit my mother and ask her what life was like for me growing up. Apparently she told him that I worked for Mr. Ben and although she didn't know his exact address, she knew about where he lived. Norman decided to drive out to that area and ask around about Mr. Ben. Said it didn't take him very long to get pointed in the direction of where Mr. Ben lived. Once he got there he introduced himself and the moment he said he was my child and told him his age, Mr. Ben's mind had already been made up. He told him about the affair me and him had around the time Norman would have been conceived.

He then showed him some pictures of when he was young and together they agreed that Norman was most likely Mr. Ben's son. I knew he was, of course I hadn't said anything to Benjamin about it and tried to sweep it under the rug for years. But even I wasn't so overzealous as to think that secret would never get out, I just never thought it would happen in the midst of me trying to fix my marriage. I asked Norman to never tell Benjamin about any of it, that if he did then it could ruin everything we had been working for the past few years. He agreed and we went about with things as usual. I never told Norman this but knowing for a fact that he was Mr. Ben's son gave me a special love for him, the kind of love that I only shared for my first child that I believe also to be from Mr. Ben. As a parent one should never pick favorites, but there's a difference when you have a baby with the man who you felt was your soulmate versus the man you were married to.

After those two issues, we had peace for a little while. Rose had given birth to another boy and Damon was done with high school and on his way to becoming an artist. I knew I had given birth to some truly anointed children because it seemed that no matter what they did or had gone through, they were true survivors of their pasts. As

Ben's other two kids grew older, they wanted to spend more personal time with him and their momma which I didn't mind. I was reminded after all that I wasn't their mother and truthfully I had plenty of my own. One day while Ben took an out of town trip with the kids and their momma, I had an unexpected visitor come by. It was Mr. T, my old bough from the years that Ben and I weren't faithful to one another.

"What are you doing here, Thomas?" I asked him.

"Coming by to see you, it's been a while," he said.

"Well, it has been. There are some things that are a bit different from the last time we saw each other."

"I see. For one, you have no bruises on your face and you're home alone."

"Well Benjamin and I have gone through a lot of marriage reconstruction and now we are doing better than we ever were. We renewed our vows and it's brought me so much peace."

"You renewed your vows to him? What made that happen? He threaten you or something?"

"No, he didn't threaten me. He confessed his love for me and changed his ways. Now everything is made new," I told him. He looked at me like I had lost my mind and gave a smirk. I hated when he smirked because I was so damn attracted to him. . He then took out a cigar, lit it, and said to me after taking a puff and blowing it away from me,

"Deborah, I've known you a long time and I've loved you for a long time. You were a patient woman for the sake of your children, but this is dangerous. Trying to fix a toxic relationship only increases its toxicity. And no amount of biblical references about redemption is going to change that."

"You don't know what you're talking about Thomas, what I have with Benjamin is something real and genuine. If you don't like it or can't understand it for some reason then you can go, the door's waiting for you." I pushed passed him and went to open the door so he could leave but he grabbed me by the arm and pulled me close to him.

"Quit acting like a diva Deborah, you're too old for that now. Be honest with yourself and go with who you really want to be with. Not someone who forces you into a false sense of happiness." After he said that I wanted to knock him out, not because he was saying something that wasn't true but because he was saying something that actually was.

"Thomas, can you please just go?"

"What's wrong? Is Ben coming home any time soon? Oh let me guess, he's off with some woman or better yet, some man right?"

"As a matter of fact he is but it's a woman that he had children with, not that it's any of your business anyway what he does"

"Having kids with anyone besides you? He's an idiot Deborah, you deserve better. You always have. I always wished I could have had children with you." I wanted so badly just to escape him, I did not want to do anything that would hurt my marriage to Benjamin any more than it already had been hurt. But I had given the devil an open door from the time I let him in that house. I had shot my own self in the foot. With the way he was holding me and staring into my eyes, I couldn't resist him. He started caressing my face and I leaned in closer to him. I kissed him and he picked me up and carried me off into the bedroom. It only took a few moments of temptation and pleasure to undo all the work that me and Benjamin had done in our marriage. And I did it without even thinking of Benjamin once.

After about a week, Benjamin finally came back home. He was in the happiest mood I had ever seen him in. Said that he had so much fun with the boys and their momma and that he wanted to do it more often. I encouraged him because who was I to tell him he shouldn't spend time with his own kids. He started touching me and I tried to tell him I wasn't in the mood. Who would be after sleeping with another man three nights in a row before their husband came home from an innocent trip with his kids? For some reason, he was insisting on us having sex so I gave it to him and shortly afterwards went to take a shower. Once I got out, I wrapped a towel around myself and was surprised to see Benjamin wasn't in the bedroom. I called for him but didn't get a response. I figured he'd probably gone out to get some food since I hadn't been shopping since he left. I put on a blouse and decided to go sit on the back porch. Ben was there, he was silent and had something bunched up in his left hand.

"Hey! I was calling for you. Did you hear me?" I asked him. He didn't respond to me, just sat there staring off into the distance and tightening the grip on what he had in his hand. I went to go place my hand on his shoulder and as I looked down I noticed what was in his hand, it was a pair of underwear. One of the pairs of underwear that Thomas had on while he was over. I tried to not react and decided to play dumb. "Are those a new pair of underwear that you bought while on the trip? I haven't seen them before." He didn't answer; he stayed silent and it was making me go crazy. I couldn't lose my marriage. "I guess maybe you already had them and I just didn't notice. Anyway, I'm going to go prepare dinner," I said as I tried to walk away.

He finally spoke. "While I was gone, all I could think of is why. Why did I even bother renewing my vows with you when I felt so free away from you? The whole time I was with the kids and their mom, I felt like I was where I really belonged. I felt loved Deborah. I don't feel that with you, I haven't for a very long time." I snapped on him immediately.

"What the hell do you mean Benjamin? I do love you."

"You pretend to but I'm not stupid Deborah. Why do you think I spent all that time cheating on you with different women and men? I was searching for a happiness that I never felt with you. When I was with them, my real family, the love in my heart came back. I was so happy that I decided to make love to Amy the whole time and I felt no guilt. Did you feel any guilt when you made love to whoever in the hell these belong to?" He threw them in my face.

I didn't know what to say at first, I couldn't believe that he not only cheated me, but told me in so many words that he didn't love me. There I was, getting my heartbroken yet again and my fantasy marriage crushed before my eyes. But I refused to fall apart unlike before, I wanted to do something to stop the problem for good. "Yes, it did feel good Benjamin. It felt good because I loved him, I love him." We stopped, he didn't say a word and neither did I. We just stared at each other, observing each other's movements and waiting to see who would react first. He then smirked, walked towards me and stared me up and down before saying,

"You're a bitch." He struck me in the face. He jumped on top of me and kept hitting me over and over while cussing me out. He kicked me until my face bled and I tried to fight him off. After he had crippled me physically, he got down and started ripping off my clothes and choking me until I couldn't breathe. He undid his pants, loosened his grip around my neck and began raping me. I didn't fight it, I wanted to but I was just too weak to. He had beaten me within an inch of my life and I just couldn't do anything about it. When he was finished he spit on me and walked away. I heard the shower turn on but I didn't move, I was still trying to gain the energy. I know what I did was horrible but it was no reason for him to treat me the way he did, there was no reason to ever treat anyone that way. I was sick of just being accustomed to it clicked in my mind that it was not only wrong, it was despicable. As I heard him get out the shower, I finally managed to get the strength to pull myself up. As I saw him walking towards the front door and carrying a suitcase with him, I went into the bedroom and searched in the closet. I found my 9mm handgun and made sure it was fully loaded. He was never going to hurt me again, I told myself that in that moment and I meant it.

With what little strength I had, I exited the house from the door of the closed off front porch just in time to see him packing his suitcase into his car. I put the gun behind my back and dragged myself close to him. .I stood at the front of the car and he stood at back. He closed the trunk and looked up and saw me.

"Don't beg me to stay Debbie, it's over. I'm taking my things, the money, and everything else with me. I refuse to spend my life being unhappy." He began walking towards the car door and I stared at him. Before he could open it, I took the gun from behind my back and pointed it directly at his head. "Deborah, what the hell? Look baby, I'll stay. Is that you want? I planned on coming back anyway, I just wanted to scare you so you can break up with that guy. You know I love you and only—"

"Fuck you nigga." I fired off three shots right to his head. His head hit the car door as he fell down to the ground. It was over, the nightmare marriage that I endured for decades was finally over. I was finally emancipated from the all the men that held me in bondage.

CHAPTER NINE

The events that I experienced that day with Benjamin would forever stick in my mind. I felt terrible about killing the father of my kids but dammit he deserved it. He seemed to think that it was okay to beat me and rape me, treat me like I was cattle or something. I wasn't going to settle though, I refused to.

After I repaid him for the damage that he did to me, I decided it was time to move on. I talked to Thomas about everything that had happened and he comforted me in the way a man should. He held me, told me I was beautiful and worth something, and tried to heal every wound I had. He would come home after a long day of work and say to me, "You were on my mind the whole day, all I could think about was coming home to the beautiful woman that I've loved since I first laid eyes on." His words always had a way of making me feel better and like my old self again. The me that I was even before my father died. Thomas had a true authentic love for me.

I knew that I would not be able to hide Ben's death from our kids. But I avoided answering the phone for about a month after the incident. Since Thomas was there, he helped me come up with a cover story once I finally talked to the kids. We told them that Ben had went out of town by himself because he wanted some time alone and that he ended up committing suicide while he was out of town. I know it was terrible to tell them a lie on such a big topic but what would they think if they knew I killed their dad? Better yet what would they think if they knew what he did to me to make me snap? The reactions to their dad's death was mixed. My first few that I had raised with Papa Joe were devastated, it was their second dad they loss. I felt terrible even breaking the news to them but I assured them we would get through it just like we had gotten through Papa Joe's death. All my kids with Benjamin took it hard too, though not as bad as the others. The only exceptions was Rose, Damon, and Benny. Rose especially was devastated because she loved him and no matter what went on between us, she was always a daddy's girl. Then there was Norman. He didn't really have a reaction to it when I told him. Only said that he was beginning to dedicate his life to God and that he'd spent his time taking care of his biological father, Mr. Ben, because he was old and starting to become ill. I wish he would've expressed more of his feelings to me but he was so distant about the situation. He didn't even bother going to the funeral. I understood, I barely wanted to go myself. Ben's body wasn't at the funeral of course, because Thomas and I had made sure we'd gotten completely rid of it. There wasn't a trace of it left and no one needed to know what actually happened to him. I couldn't risk anyone going to the police and telling them about it and I only write it now because even if someone reads it and reports me, I'll be safe from harm. After all my memory is beginning to fade away as I write this and I know that my time is almost up.

There was one other person I ended up telling about what I had done to Benjamin: Rose. She was our baby girl and even though she had three kids at that point with a fourth on the way, I knew she needed to know the truth. I sat her down one day and talked to her, told her about the whole situation. I took it all the way back to when I had first caught Benjamin screwing the man he claimed was his cousin back when we were in the early stages of our relationship. Reason I told her is because she had seen some of the violence with me and Benjamin more than her siblings. Because of that, I figured she'd be able to understand, and luckily she did. She wasn't upset with me nor did she blame me for what I had done. She said to me, "Momma, I grew up watching you two fight like two men. I never understood it and I didn't like it, but it was all I knew. As much as I loved daddy, I know that you and him didn't love each other the way you should have. Had it not been for Pete, I wouldn't know true love."

Pete was her husband who was six years her junior. I admired him for taking on children that weren't biologically his, but I treated him like I hated him. Every chance I got, I showed him how much I didn't like him. Looking back, I think that's what eventually drove Rose away from me. I didn't mean to treat her husband so terribly but I just couldn't stand anything about his personality, he was so soft and sensitive. I didn't understand why my daughter couldn't have chosen a man with more backbone, one who would actually act like a man and not some sensitive teenager. But beyond his sensitivity, there was a deeper reason why treated him that way. I was jealous, my daughter had the kind of relationship that I wish I could've had. Pete respected her and treated her like she was his queen, he worshipped the ground she walked on. I couldn't get Benjamin to do that for me, he just saw me as disposable. Of course I had Thomas and he treated me well but I eventually found myself annoyed by him. He never wanted to fight me, physically or otherwise. He always wanted to go on dates, he was very big on romance. But I didn't have no interest in all that anymore, that part of me had died along with Benjamin. I thought I wanted Thomas but outside of sex, he didn't do anything at all for me and after a while even that became repetitive. It wasn't rough like it was with Benjamin, there was no power play or struggle. He just always wanted things clean and nice, but I wasn't a clean and nice person. I got tired of his "gentleman" behavior and filed for divorce. It's a shame really because he hadn't done anything wrong necessarily, he just wasn't who I really wanted to be with. He had all the right behaviors, but he it was simply coming from the wrong person. Or maybe the real truth is by the time Thomas and I had finally fallen in love, I was already too far gone. My dreams were dead at that point and there was no purpose in attempting to revive them.

The years following that brought about some sense of peace, if you can call it that. Truthfully I didn't really know the meaning of that word but I knew that at least I didn't have to put up with a man or anyone else being in my life for that matter. My children did make it a note to visit me, particularly when they needed something. I always gave what I had of course because I was getting old and what was I going to do with it anyway? At that point, my life had become completely revolved around helping my kids out whenever they asked, getting to see all of my grandkids and great grandkids, and going to work. My job was exactly what I had always done, personal care for older white people. It seemed like I had such a strong tie to them my whole life and honestly they had always looked out for me even more than my own race. I would also occasionally take trips back home to Alabama to see my mother and my siblings but that usually didn't last very long. I had become notorious for being the different person in the family, the one that had chosen to leave Alabama and start a new life in Florida, and they made it known when I went back home. I felt uncomfortable sometimes by how country they were, like they were stuck in the early 1900s while we were all living in the 90's.

I remember having a deep conversation with my mother about everything I had done, everything I had been through in my life. It was a breakthrough moment for us. She held me and told me, "Deborah, I'm sorry if you thought I didn't love you when your father died. Life all around me seemed to start moving so quickly but I didn't feel like I was moving at all. I love you baby girl, God blessed me with you and I couldn't be more grateful for it. I'm sorry I didn't show it like I should have." She held me and I cried into her arms. Boy did we probably look strange that day, two old women holding one another and crying. But I didn't care how strange it may have looked, she was my mother and after so long of not knowing where my relationship stood with her, it felt good to get a moment of peace and deliverance between us.

Around 1998, I got a phone call that I didn't see coming. Apparently my baby boy Damon had been driving and had somehow gotten into a car accident. I rushed to the hospital, praying along the way. I kept telling God, "Please don't take him Lord, please don't take my little boy." Damon was in his 30's at that time and far from being a little boy, but to a parent, the baby will always be the baby. When I got to the hospital I was told he was in the OR, and he had to have emergency surgery done due to the extensive damage he had on his face. I called his siblings and they all showed up to give their support. There's nothing more powerful than having a family that bands together in times of tragedy. The love and prayers that we brought to the hospital that night deepened my faith. Damon came out of the surgery alive after being in there for over 5 hours. When the doctor came to me to give me the good news, I almost leaped for joy.

But his good news came with a catch, as most tidbits of good news usually do. He told me that because of the damage done to him, Damon needed to have cosmetic surgery on his face. I was quick to tell him yes but he explained that the surgery costs around $500,000. That was a lot of money for me and the years had caused me to lose a lot of my inheritance that Papa Joe had left. It didn't matter though, I was determined to pay for the surgery. I gave the doctor the permission to do it and told him it would be paid in full. I then rushed home and began making phone calls to every white person I had ever worked for. One thing to note about working for white people is that they were very generous to you if you took good care of them. I had some donate $10,000, others $50,000. They were willing to help and I couldn't have been more appreciative. But even after making ten phone calls, I was still $250,000 short of what I needed.

I prayed to God about finding me an answer, then it dropped in my spirit: Mr. Ben. He was the only person I hadn't contacted and purposefully since he was nearing the age of 80 at that time. The last I heard about him was from Norman and he said his health wasn't good but that was over

10 years ago. Even though I had periodically talked to Norman, he never brought up Mr. Ben in our conversations. Since Norman didn't show up to the hospital, I figured I'd give him call. "Hello? Norman, it's me, your mother. I was wondering if you had any contact with your father lately."

"Yes I have, why do you want to know?"

"It's a long story but I need to talk to him about something regarding money" I said desperately.

"Money? Mom if you need money, then just ask me, I can lend you some."

"Not what I need Norman, this is a large amount. $250,000 to be exact."

"What do you need that kind of money for? What's going on?"

"Look Norman, I can't answer all your questions. I don't have time for that right now, I did leave you a voicemail about Damon. If you want the full story listen to the voicemail but right now I need your dad's number." He grew quiet for a minute and I thought he had hung up. Then, he came out of his silence and gave me the number. I called immediately but didn't get an answer. Waited an hour, tried calling again, and still no answer. I had to come up with something else, I wasn't going to sit around and just wait for him to call me back, I needed to get to him, and quickly. I hopped in my car and sped down the interstate. I got to Alabama in half the time it normally takes to get there. I went straight to Mr. Ben's house and banged on the door so hard I'm surprised I didn't break it.

After about a couple of minutes, he answered. He studied me for a minute and gave me that same old smile he had every time he saw me. "Deborah? I don't believe it." he said.

"It's me, mind if I come in?" I asked. He didn't say anything, just smiled and let me in. I was surprised when I walked in, the house looked so different. I didn't know if he ever remarried so I wasn't sure what to expect considering his age, but I was pleasantly surprised. It was clean, almost as clean as when I used to work for him.

"Your face, you look surprised. Let me guess, didn't think the house would be clean did you?"

"No I didn't but I'm happy to see it is. Did you get remarried or something?"

"I didn't, no need to. The woman I loved had moved away to Florida so I spent my life focused on my work and my family. Specifically our son." I can't say I was too surprised that he brought Norman up, after all we had never really had a conversation about him.

"He told me he'd been spending time with you. Wait, did he clean the house for you?"

"He did, he's a very gifted young man. The perfect combination of his parents if I do say so myself."

"I know I should have told you about him a long time ago but I didn't know how to. At first I wasn't sure then when I was, I just decided to let it go."

"Deborah, I'm 78 years old. I have nothing to be upset about, I understand why you did what you did. I understand you were going through a marriage, a tough one from what I hear. I do have one question though, is Norman the only one?"

I shook my head. "No, my oldest is yours too. I wasn't sure for a while but he looks even more like you than Norman." He smirked, I think it made him as happy as it made me to know that we shared kids together.

"So we have two kids together? Well, at least I know who I'll give the property to when I pass."

"That's what I'm here to talk to you about, not the farm but it does involve getting something from you."

He joked, "I'm an old man Deborah, I can make love still but it might take me a little longer to get me started than it used to."

I laughed. "Actually I was going to ask you for some money." He smiled then walked towards the table in his living room. He picked up a check and handed it to me. It was for $250,000 and it was made out to me. I was confused at first but then I figured Norman must have contacted him before I had gotten there.

"Norman told me that you needed it for his brother. I didn't ask any questions, even though he kept acting as if he had to persuade me. I told him that you were the greatest love of my life, there is nothing that you can ask for that I wouldn't give to you. I also put a little extra in there specifically for you."

"Thank you Mr. Ben, I wish there was a way I could repay you." He grabbed my hand and looked at me like we were young again. It felt so good, we hugged one another and kissed. "The best thing you can do is go take care of your family, I love you always Deborah."

"I love you too, thank you for this. Thank you." After one more kiss, I told him I had to go. My heart felt like it was simultaneously uplifted and in sorrow. I had always known that what I had with Mr. Ben was something much more powerful than what I had with Benjamin or anyone else for that matter. The fact is that I wish I would have chosen Mr. Ben back when I knew

Benjamin was fooling around with other guys, but I stuck with someone who was no good for me. Benjamin was not the one for me but it didn't matter. I wouldn't have had some of my most beloved kids had I not married him so I had no room for regret.

After the surgery, Damon was physically back to normal, other than the scar he had on his face. Mentally however, he was in a slow decline. He had started having nightmares where he relived the events of the accident. It became so bad that I had him move in with me. I had a small apartment-like building built for him on the property so he could have his privacy and such, but I kept going out to check on him. It wasn't cheap to give him his own place but I used the "little extra" that Mr. Ben gave me to pay for it. I would periodically go and check on Norman and every time I did, I saw his condition worsen. He began drinking and doing heavy drugs. His anger began to get out of control. I didn't know what to do with him. He was my son, my baby boy and yet I had no idea how to comfort him. That brought our relationship to a strain as I watched him slowly slip away. I felt like I had somehow failed him as a mother and that guilt made my own mental state worsen along with his.

About a year later, my daughter Rose had to move in. She'd gotten a divorce and had been diagnosed with HIV that was progressively becoming AIDS. It didn't matter to me how she contracted it, though I originally thought it was from Pete. I just wanted to take care of my daughter and show her that I loved her. The main hurdle to jump was her moving in meant I had two of my children to worry about. Two who were going through more trauma than I could imagine. And along with those two kids, I had Rose's four kids to take care of as well. I didn't mind of course but all I could think of is how I was supposed to take care of all of these people by myself at my age. I knew I was biting off more than I could chew but if I didn't do it then who was going to? My other children would come by the house and help when they could but I ended up having to help them too, financially.

To make matters worse, it was no breeze taking care of Rose. I don't know if it was because her father was gone or she was heartbroken from her divorce but she seemed completely uninterested in taking her medication. I pleaded with her every day to take it, even yelled at her like she was some kind of child. But it didn't make a difference, she would act like she took the medication, then spat it out once I left the room. Having all of these things going on at once is what led to my steady mental decline. How could I take care of myself when everyone else in my life needed to be taken care of?

The beginning of the millennium didn't prove to be any easier on me. Things actually worsened in the following years. First Rose passed away in 2000, leaving me devastated. My youngest daughter, the apple of my eye, was gone forever. The conditions that she left under caused a bitterness that I admittedly took out on her children who were under my care. I was so angry with her for not taking care of herself, for letting herself just slowly waste away until there was nothing left of her. I didn't let go of that anger though I desperately needed to.

Adding on to my pain and bitterness, my mother passed away a year after Rose. Being that our relationship was complicated, I didn't know how to process her death. I was hurt beyond words of course, but it went much further than that. Its one thing to lose a person that you're close with, at least then you have good memories to look back on. But I left my mother, my siblings, and my whole life behind when I left Alabama. And because my mother had apologized for her unintentional neglect, I felt so much guilt for how I left them. I felt like when daddy died, he'd left me in charge to take care of them. I was the most responsible and the most willing, but I was too caught up in my own life and ended up neglecting them. I did the same thing to my family that I had complained my mother did to me. Going over all those thoughts in my mind diminished my faith. I kept telling myself that the good Lord didn't love me as much The Bible claimed He did and eventually, I stopped going to church and used work as an excuse. It may be sad to say but at that point, but I had begun to accept that the rest of my life wasn't going to go well. I was a woman in her retirement years working 15 hours a day to take care of four kids and one adult.

If happiness was in my life, it was only feigned or fleeting at best. I accepted that I had my happy season in my life long ago when I was with Mr. Ben and it was long gone, never to return.

CHAPTER TEN

I spent my next few years raising Rose's kids the best I could, all things considered. Even if they had all been perfect kids, I don't think it would have made things any better for them or me. Like I said, I was bitter at Rose for how she left and I constantly took it out on her kids. Her eldest moved out in 2002, he decided to join the Navy. But he was strongly independent during the small amount of time he lived with me that he was barely a problem. After his mother's death, he didn't want to talk much and spent all his time working and chasing after girls. Besides his personal life,

I will say that he did well watching after his younger siblings. I worked overnight and so couldn't be around all the time like I should have.

Like I've mentioned before, I know they say you shouldn't pick favorites when it comes to children but I had mine. It was the middle boy, he reminded me so much of the good sides of Benjamin. He was tall and very intelligent, had the biggest smile, and stayed to himself a lot. Just like Benjamin he liked to build things and spent most of his time with his computers and video games. I never found any real fault in him, I guess because I was so focused on his good sides.

The two younger siblings weren't afforded that same treatment. Looking back on it now, I hate how I treated them. They probably went on with their lives thinking that I had no love for them but that wasn't the case. It was just that every time I saw them, all I could think about was Rose. They were the most like her and I loved it and at the same time, treated them unfairly for it. The only girl of the bunch, Keisha, always got into it with me, as she had a smart mouth and was fiercely opinionated, just like her mother. The only difference was I was too busy being caught up with Benjamin to go after Rose when she was younger the way I went after Keisha.

Our relationship was so tumultuous.
I remember one day I was walking through
the backyard and happened to step in some
dog crap. I don't know what got into me but
I took my shoe off, slapped Keisha with it
and told her to clean it up. I know I shouldn't
have treated her the way I did but I was
honestly out of control. Weighed down by
everything I had been through and had not
had the chance to deal with my issues
properly. Honestly I didn't know *how* to deal
with it properly. It's not like I had
counseling or something when I had lost my
dad at a young age or was forced to touch
Papa Joe when I was younger, I just dealt
with everything as it came. If you keep

going from trauma to trauma instead of glory to glory, you begin to build up the characteristics and the attitude of a traumatic person. The truth is that I was in no condition to be taking care of kids, they would have been better off going into foster care. You cannot take care of other people, when you haven't properly taken care of yourself. I know now that not healing from my past issues is what got me to where I am, but the damage to my family and my own self has already been done. If Jesus is real, I am in need of His redemption before this disease ends what's left of my life.

Out of all of Rose's children, there was one that I wish I had at least shown more appreciation to. Her youngest, Dion. He was Pete's child, meaning that he had a strike against him before he was even born. As I said before, I was no fan of Pete and that in combination with how I felt about Rose, influenced how I treated Dion. "Dion! Get your ass in here right now!" I would always say to him. "Yes ma'am," he always would reply. He was so obedient, even when I gave him every reason not to be. It seemed unfair, and truly it was, but I relied on him to do everything for me. It was a strain to get the others to help, at least without some type of back talk or complaint. But Dion didn't complain, at least not to my face. He was always so dead set on helping me with everything, cooking, cleaning, and maintaining my garden just to name a few.

It was a change for me having to be so dependent on someone but my physical health was beginning to decline. I wasn't sick or anything but I had issues walking and after an emergency doctor visit, discovered I had ruptured discs in my lower back. Can you imagine how that made me feel? Going from being a woman who was fiercely independent to an old woman who had to depend on a child to take care of her. It angered me that life was putting me in the position of dependency and I tried to fight it, but you can't fight what God has spoken. I found that out the hard way in 2004 when a hurricane hit the entire Gulf Coast causing catastrophic damage. Many homes were destroyed, businesses closed, and lives were lost. My home was fine other than some leaking and minor damage, at least compared to people around me. But my workplace was destroyed and so was my ability to work. I had driven to work that evening before the storm had gotten bad so I could take care of Ms. Blanche, the older woman under my care. But the building collapsed while I was at work and I almost injured myself in my attempt to get to my car so I could get back home. Ms. Blanche passed away when the building fell but luckily I did make it out safely. I was happy to see all of the kids were safe when I got home but that night marked a change in my life. A change for the worse.

Because I was no longer working, I had more time to be at home. That meant more time with the kids, and more time to think about where I was in my life. My demand on the kids due to my increased dependency became too much for them to handle. "Dion! I need you to come clean my room! Then I want you to clean the living room, scrub the kitchen floor, and water the plants outside!" I know he was tired of me giving him a list of things to do every day, but what other choice did I have? I couldn't do the work myself and he was the most available resource around, still I know that was part of what drove him and his siblings away from me.

One day I had taken it too far with my demanding attitude. I called him into my room to rub my feet with some alcohol and a washcloth. He kept rubbing soft like I was some fragile old lady and it triggered something inside of me. "Give me that damn rag, nigga! You rub like a sissy!" I told him as I slapped him with the cloth. The look on his face told me that he was no longer doing things for me because he wanted to, he was doing them because he was afraid of me and what I would do to him if he didn't do it. He started acting like what I complained about being for so long, a slave. It hadn't clicked in me at that time but I had passed down the same curse that was on me to him. I was slowly destroying both his spirit and his character.

About a year after that, I got a call home from school one day about Dion. It was unusual for me to get calls about him since he was typically a good student. His teacher claimed that he was in class running around, chasing some female. I said to myself that was it, I had enough issues to deal with and didn't need to add a bad kid along with the rest of what I had going on. Not being able to work or do anything for myself, dealing with Keisha and how she would run away and come back as she pleased, dealing with Damon and his addictions, so much pressure had been building on me. Years of dealing with these things were attacking my mind but I was ready to get rid of the stress. It was like the bondage that I thought I got rid of when I got Benjamin out of my life had come back to haunt me, just in a different form.

When Dion got home from school that day I had a talk with him. "I heard you were running around in school today chasing some girl in class,"

"No ma'am, who told you that?"

"Nigga, I know you ain't gone sit here and lie right to my face. See, that's your problem. You ain't nothing but a liar, just like your damn father, you lie! But that's okay, I'm about to beat the lies out of you. Now go strip your clothes off down to your underwear and come back here so I can beat your ass." I remember the look in his eyes, he was terrified. I hated seeing that look but I needed to show him that his behavior in school was unacceptable. At least that's the excuse that I gave myself so I wouldn't feel bad about what I was about to do.

I beat his ass so bad that day that his skin was almost bursting with blood. I studied his body and noticed he had red marks, pink marks, and purple marks all over his arms and his body. I had beaten kids before, all of my kids and even his siblings. But the way I beat him that day said something to me, that wasn't discipline, it was my attempt at catharsis. The last time I had beaten a kid that severely is when Benjamin was alive and even then, he was there to get me to stop eventually. It didn't matter to me that I had just beaten the person who took care of me, I was just relieved that I finally got out all of the anger that I felt on the inside. The Deborah James

that had been raped and beaten and cheated

on felt justified. When I beat my grandson, I

wasn't beating *him*. I was beating all the

issues that I ever had in my life. I was

beating Benjamin for how he treated me in

our marriage, Papa Joe for introducing me to

sex at an early age, my mother for not loving

me properly when my father died, the man

who infected Rose with HIV. I was beating

all of those demons, Dion was just the

vessel.

The next day after I beat him,

indignation came knocking at my front door.

I knew that my grandson was different than

his siblings and much more different than his aunts and uncles. What I didn't expect is for him to call the police on me. It was ironic for me because I had done so many other things in my life that I could have been arrested for, but I never expected to get arrested for child abuse. But it happened and I had no one to blame but myself. I was responsible for what was happening to me because I didn't know how to control my anger and frustration. There was nothing in the world more humiliating than getting hauled off to jail for beating a 12 year old, especially my own grandson. I suffered that day and going forward. I didn't have a heavy sentence by the grace of God, but I did have a bail set at $50,000. There was no way I could pay it and I was almost sure that Mr. Ben had passed away by then, but I had just not been told about it. But thank God for my children, Benny paid my bail and got me out. I was free, physically, but spiritually I was dead. When I got back home, Dion was gone and had been placed with my firstborn, the other child that I had conceived with Mr. Ben, so I knew he was in good hands. I wasn't allowed to see him without supervision and I was no longer allowed to be around any children. I had destroyed not only my greatest servant and assistance, but also my family. My kids never said it but I knew those events made them look at me differently. Yes, I did beat them in a similar manner, but the extent was never paid much attention to because they never called the police on me. They would have never thought to do such a thing because I was their mother and back when I raised them, it was common to be able to beat your kids however bad you wanted. The 2000's were a different time, there were new laws and regulations and I had to come out of my old way of thinking. But because I didn't, I suffered consequences for my ignorance that would follow me the rest of my life.

CHAPTER ELEVEN

A couple of years after Dion was removed, his siblings followed his lead. All of Rose's kids had gone and it was only me and Damon left in that house. Damon was usually gone and living his life the way he'd been living it since the accident. I was left in the house to pretty much fend for myself with little help and hardly the mobility to do so. Those years before I ended up here were hard. It seemed that all of the things I had done or tried to sweep under the rug in my life came back to haunt me. It started when my son Norman came to see me one day while I was at the house alone.

"Momma, I need to talk to you about something important." That line alone scared me, when Norman said that it always lead to something big. "I don't know how to say this but when I was younger, it wasn't just daddy that raped me. Benny did too." I didn't know Norman to lie, but I refused to believe that Benny would do anything like that to his own brother.

"Norman, you must be confused. Your brother would never do nothing like that to you, he don't like men no way. He has a wife."

"Daddy had a wife too momma, it never stopped him. Why would you think I would lie about something like this? I'm your son and for years you have treated me like I didn't really matter to you. Is it because I'm Mr. Ben's son and not daddy's? Or maybe you just had it out for me since the moment you carried me."

"Norman, why would you think that? For one, I loved Mr. Ben more than I've ever loved anyone in my life. I just think you a bit confused, your brother don't mess with no boys for one and two, you are his brother. He would never do anything like that to hurt you." He began crying, I remember hearing the desperation in his voice as he cried but I couldn't accept what he said. I loved my Benny, I wasn't gonna let him make him look bad. "Norman listen, I think you're confused or you might have had a dream or something. Now you can take that story you're telling and put it down in a book or something 'cause that's as far as its going. No one touched you ever in your life and I don't want to hear you lie through your teeth anymore about it, understand?"

"No one ever touched me? Momma did you forget what Ben did to me? Oh let me guess, you don't believe that happened either do you? You don't believe anything your children tell you and that's what you're in the condition you're in now! Whether you accept it or not, you know the truth. But don't expect me to be here when you need someone to take care of you. You reap what you sow and all you've sown with me is rejection, but you don't have to believe me 'cause God does. And as long as He's my witness, I have everything I need." That was all I heard him say as he stormed out of the house. I felt so guilty, did I just deny one of my children the cross they bared? If so, what kind of mother was I? Is this the real reason that I find myself having to write me story down because I hope to have some kind of mercy and forgiveness from not only God, but all the family members that I know I failed.

Some time later, I received another visitor. It was my granddaughter, Jayla. Her mother was one of my older children by Papa Joe, Harriet. Harriet and I were close, although she seemed disconnected every time she came around. I think she was dissatisfied with the way she was raised, how I would give Benjamin all my attention and casted my kids to the side. She held on to whatever pain she had from her childhood and how I treated her. I cared, of course, but there was only so much I could do for a grown adult holding on to the past, I had my own pain to handle.

Her daughter Jayla was in her 30's and was such a beautiful woman with a free spirit. She reminded me so much of Rose in some ways so I had a special place in my heart for her. When she visited me she said she needed to talk to me about something important. I was tired of hearing "important" topics from anyone in my family, every time they claimed something to be important, it always turned out to be something tragic instead.

"Granny, first I was wondering how you have been doing."

"I've been fine dear, not much to do these days except watch TV. How about you and the kids?"

"We've been fine, maintaining like always."

"Well that's good. So what's up? What did you have to tell me?" I wanted to get whatever she had to say out, I knew there was a reason she was stalling and my patience had dwindled considerably with my age and time."

"Well…." She stopped for a second. I could tell that whatever she had to tell me had to have been something serious because she began to tear up so bad she couldn't even get the words out. Seeing her like that softened my heart and made me reach out to try to hug her for comfort.

"Jayla, you know you can tell me anything. I'm your grandmother and I do love you with all of my heart, talk to me"

"It's about Uncle Benny." Her voice sounded so fragile, so full of fear when she said his name. My anxiety began to rise, I was praying in my heart she wasn't going to tell me something similar to what Norman said to me. I couldn't take another false accusation about my son

"He….he touched me when I was younger. I wanted to say something to you about it a long time ago granny but I didn't know how to come to you about it. I'm sorry." Her tears were streaming down her face like a waterfall at that point. I felt some sense of compassion for her, but it didn't override what I knew to be true about my Benny. He may have had his flaws, but I knew he would never do anything like what he was being accused of.

"Did Norman put you to this?" 'Cause if he did…"

"What? Granny no, Norman doesn't have anything to do with this. This is about what I went through, please tell me you don't think I would lie about something like this. I didn't think she was lying, I knew she was and it was infuriating me. I reached behind a pillow on the couch behind me and pulled out a knife.

"Listen Jayla, I don't like making threats to people. But when you come after someone I love, especially one of my own children, I have to let you know that it's not the thing you want to do. Do me a favor, forget everything you just told me. Go in the bathroom, dry your eyes, and show yourself out of my house. And if I hear from anyone else that you've been spreading this lie about my boy, I will kill you. You understand?"

"I understand granny, but you hear me when I tell you this. You can't protect him forever, your days are numbered. You can threaten me, do whatever you want to anyone else, but the truth is still the truth."

She walked away and left after her little speech, but I wasn't scared of affected. I meant what I said about my Benny, I believed in his innocence and even now I still do.

I couldn't stand the thought of people disrespecting my son or talking about him like he was some kind of sex crazed demon. I knew my Benney hadn't done the things they were trying to tell me, I believed he didn't. I figured that maybe they had all heard about what happened to him in 7th grade and were trying to pick at my son out of jealousy.

Besides the lies coming to me about son, I suffered other personal losses. I saw my garden slowly wither away. Without Dion there to tend to it, there was no one who was willing to take care of it. I tried the best I could, but I fell into such a deep depression that I honestly stopped caring about anything. I lost the motivation to walk or take adequate care of myself, and I fought my kids on trying to take me to the doctor. I understood that they were only trying to help but I kept telling myself I didn't need a doctor. I had spent my whole life fixing my own health when I got sick. Any sickness could be cured with a good pot of collard greens, some habanero peppers, and some faith. I just knew that I had it all figured out and that I would be able to handle everything myself. But if that were the case, I wouldn't be writing this from what I consider to be my deathbed. The truth is, all those beliefs I had about not going to the doctors and such was the result of the poisonous mindset that had developed in me after my father's passing. If wisdom had laid that revelation upon me when I was in my prime then maybe some things could have been avoided, but everything happens for a purpose that is bigger than what we can see. I still haven't figured out what's the purpose in what I had to go through but God allows us to see things when it's time.

My biggest and final blow that forced me into a nursing home was when Damon moved out. He was the only person I had physically with me on a somewhat consistent basis. Some of the other kids would occasionally visit but Damon lived with me. Even if it was hard to get him to do stuff for me sometimes, he was still the only one physically around. I relied on my baby boy, my sweet baby boy that I loved so dearly, to take care of me. I loved my son with everything in me and though he saw me go through some of the worst things, he still hardened his heart towards me. I write these words in both bitterness and pain because I clung unto him. It feels as though my dependency meant nothing to him, or maybe he just grew tired of me. He took my car, what little money I had left, and abandoned me. He did it without warning and seemingly without remorse. I was left with a broken heart and emptiness. That was the last straw, I had lost my parents, my husband, my grandchildren, my favorite daughter, and my baby boy. I took a moment and thought about all these things and considered suicide. What did I have to live for anyway? I had kids who were alive sure, but they didn't want anything to do with me. I had no significant other nor did I have the compassion left in me for one. I had gained so much weight over the years and treated my health so poorly that I no longer could function like a regular human being. My blood pressure was sky high, I could barely walk, I couldn't even bathe myself. It was like a curse had been placed on me when I was younger and it got worse as the years went on. I knew there was no way to stop the continuous downhill roll that I had taken. I was about ready to crash into a tree and fall into a million pieces. No person should feel that way in their senior citizen years. I thought The Bible said that your latter days will be better than your former but that wasn't the case for me. My latter days had only brought me an indescribable darkness and confliction that felt impossible to escape. The emancipation I had declared for myself decades ago when I left Alabama had only proved itself to be one big farce. There was no emancipation; in fact I was in an even worse captivity than I was before. I knew that I had finally reached the point of no return. The worst part about it all is that I had no one to blame but myself for my bondage, the real person I was in bondage to my whole life was my own flaws and sinful nature.

CHAPTER TWELVE

I now write this chapter in the present tense as it is currently the story I'm experiencing. My life has taken a complete pause after I crashed and burned a few months ago. I'm living in a senior nursing home where I have no one but a roommate. Everyone is gone now and I must deal with the cards I've been dealt like I had done so many times in the past. The only difference is this time I had nowhere to run and no one to unleash my anger and disappointment out on except my nurses. It goes without saying that I'm not very well-liked here. It may seem harsh to them that I purposely make their jobs harder than they need to be but if they were me they would do the same thing. These young women don't know what it's like to be someone who has spent her life beaten, hurt, raped, abandoned, cheated on, made to feel like I am even lower than the dirt on the ground. They don't know what it's like to spend your entire life taking care of people only to be abandoned and left to handle a brain-deteriorating disease that you don't even know how to control or what you could have done to avoid it. No, they don't know what it's like to be me. I pray that no one knows what it's like to be sick and to feel like a failure. They don't deserve this feeling, I don't even deserve it because I haven't done anything to hurt anyone. I've been told by some people who come by claiming to be my children that I hurt them but it's hard for me to believe a stranger telling me that. How can I hurt someone that I don't even know? People keep coming by this hospital room or whatever this is and telling me different things that don't make any sense. They've been telling me that I let them get hurt in unimaginable ways. I wouldn't do that though, I wouldn't let someone get hurt and not do anything about it. I'm a good person, I am. These strangers who come by keep telling me lies to stress me out. They don't realize that I'm only a fifteen year girl. I don't have any kids or anything like that. I am in a secret relationship with a man named Mr. Ben and even though I pray to marry him one day, that don't mean we're married already. Besides, how could I marry Mr. Ben when he's married and I've been secretly going behind his back to sleep with Papa Joe every time I leave the house? Oh how I wish I could tell Mr. Ben the truth, I mean I do love him without a doubt. But I've known Papa Joe my whole life and he is the man I lost my virginity to. Sure he's a little bit older but there's something so attractive about an older white man who has money and power. And I'm not just talking about the power that Mr. Ben has. Papa Joe has real power, he's Mr. Ben's boss after all and God knows I love a man with power. I never told anyone else this but I secretly have been trying to have a baby with Papa Joe. I know that if I can give birth to one of his then I will be set for life. That way I will never have to worry about anything else ever again, I will finally be able to live comfortable. I know it sounds like a conniving thing to do but it isn't like I'm having trying to have a baby by someone I don't care about. I care greatly for Papa Joe, I just also happen to care for what he can provide for me as well. And as far as

Mr. Ben goes, well I would marry him but

he isn't going to leave his wife. He may

barely talk to her and bother to even

acknowledge when she's home but he will

not leave her. I've cried my eyes out so

many nights praying that he finally would

leave her but he isn't going to. By societal

standards, it makes more sense that he's

married to her any way. He's white, she's

white. I'm just a negro and no matter what I

say or do, I'm never gone mean as much to a

white man as a white woman does. No, they

only see me as being good for what I can

give them in the bedroom and someone to

sneak off with when they want to have a

little fun. That's all I am to any of them so I figure, hell, I might as well use them too. The day will come where I can be free of all this worry and I'll find someone who truly loves me for me. I want him to be tall, brown skinned, and very intelligent. Lord knows I would give him the world and more if I can. It don't matter if what he does wrong, I'll always forgive him and give all of myself to him. I'll have more kids by him than I can keep track of and he'll treat me like a real queen. I will stay married to him no matter what until death itself separates us. I pray for a man like that every day and I know that one day God will bring him to me. When God brings my prayers to fruition and gives me the desires of my heart, I will live eternally in His glory. It'll be me, my husband, and all of our kids living in peace together. None of us will be slaves nor any kind of indentured servants. We will live forever free, forever emancipated.

EPILOGUE

Some of the greatest stories ever told in history have some of the most tragic endings: take almost any episode of the TV show "The Twilight Zone" for example. In every episode of that show an incredible story is told, but unfortunately almost every episode ends in tragedy. It always broke my heart when I would watch the show as a child sitting in my grandma's house because

I always hoped that somehow the characters would get the victory that they were working desperately for.

Hello, my name is Dion James. I'm Deborah James's grandson for anyone who's reading this diary, or book if you will. I ran across this while visiting my grandma in the nursing home one day. Apparently she had been writing in this not too long before she passed away. It saddens me in many ways because I had a very deep love for my grandmother. I feel as though my love for her would come as a surprise to her due to the way she treated me for most of my life. Yes, she did abuse me and despite me taking care of her, she never really seemed to appreciate it. It was hard dealing with someone who always made you to feel insignificant, who used every opportunity possible to attack you just because she was angry about other things in her life. As a child, I didn't really understand why she treated me the way she did, yet even still I loved her to the moon and back. That's why I don't hold it against her, honestly it would be pointless in doing so now.

As I've seen from my grandmother, it does a person no good to hold on to emotions that are supposed to die when the person dies. I think that holding on is a big reason that my grandmother ended up suffering as much as she did. She held on to her father's death and it controlled every decision in her life. There's no way I figured that out on my own, how could I? I only figured it out because I read this gem of a book she left behind. Reading it explains so much about why she acted the way she did while I was younger. She had a whole life 60 years before I was even thought about. A life that didn't seem to treat her very fairly, at least as far she documented. I don't say that because I don't believe her, it's just that she had dementia during the time that she wrote the book while in the nursing home. It makes me wonder how accurate some of the details of her past was. Was she just trying to justify her actions that she committed against everyone else? I'm unsure. It would make some sense, especially if she felt overwhelmed by guilt, but somehow I believe her. Maybe it's because I'm her grandson or because I feel sorry for her.

My grandmother couldn't have been lying about the things that she's been through, she was a true survivor. I admire her in that aspect and I hope that sharing her story with the world means something to someone out there. I pray to God that someone shows mercy on my grandmother and gives her story the chance it needs to be heard by many because I'm convinced that if it is, then it will change people's hearts. Many people have become so distant with their family because of some past trauma or hurt that was never properly addressed. I'm not trying to sound like I'm enabling bad behavior in families, nor am I saying that a person should be so quick to forget what happened to them, I certainly wasn't. I am saying though that people should be willing to forgive each other the way I've been able to forgive my grandmother and the way Christ has forgiven us for those who believe in Him. Of course in saying that I understand that it won't be an easy task for everyone, not everyone is fortunate enough to find a written recorded account of their abuser(s) or perpetrator(s) life. The chances of that even happening are low I imagine and had I not found this one, things would have been different for me. I'm not so sure I would be such an advocate for forgiveness the way I am. But because I have run into this, I feel as though I have a responsibility to share this gospel with the world. After all, what good is it to go through hell if you don't take it and turn it into something productive? Something that can heal not only you but the hundreds of thousands of others out there who have probably suffered the same way you have or possibly even worse. You have to put yourself out there, give up your story and let it be something bigger than what you went through.

Imagine if my grandmother had just one story to read or someone who talked to her about her past, her life could have taken a complete turnaround. But she never got that chance, it's almost like she died in her sins in a sense. Don't get me wrong, I know she had some measure of faith at some point in her life, but I don't think she ever really experienced true deliverance. If she had then she probably still be here today. Her mind wouldn't have started to deteriorate from all the secrets and bitterness that she was keeping to herself. I don't mean to say that every person with Alzheimer's has done something wrong, it's a disease of the mind so it's practically unpredictable. But I am a true believer in The Bible which states that you reap what you sow. She sowed a lot of bad seeds that were only poisonous to her and her future. In terms, she reaped a life where everyone she ever loved or idolized abandoned her. Nevertheless she does have me who not only pleaded for mercy for her before God, but also intends to make sure that her pain meant something. The emancipation that she spoke about in the last chapter of her book when it was clear that the Alzheimer's disease had taken her back to a much younger version of herself, is what I want to grant her. She deserves that emancipation that she spoke so faithfully about but never achieved. Even if it's the last thing that I ever do, I am making it my life's goal to make sure that she gets this freedom from bondage. That way I will know for sure that she will live a good and free life in Heaven. Her pain will be no more and her rest will be eternal. Don't worry grandma, I will do everything in my power to redeem you.

AFTERWORD

Thank you to everyone who took the time to read this book. It definitely was not an easy book to write and the process of getting everything together has been enduring to say the least. Some of you who are close to me know that this book was originally developed for two reasons. One, because I am in the process of making a movie based off the book and I wanted to generate a fan base by getting people familiar with the story. Two, the most important reason, I wrote it because God told me to. Sounds weird right? No I'm not some crazy person that hears voices in my head (other than the characters that I create). I just happen to be in the process of building my relationship with God and finding what exactly He has called me to do in this life. I know that part of why God put me here was to tell stories, specifically the stories of those who don't have an outlet to share their "gospel" with the world. It is for that reason that I prefer telling stories that may seem a little dark to some people but in actuality they talk about the complex reality that real people experience. Life is never as black and white as we'd like it to be, neither are we as people. All of us have the capability of doing some pretty horrible things, like Deborah. But we also are able to come out of the dark and go into the glorious light that comes from God. I want anyone who reads this book to consider this fact; no matter how much someone may have hurt you, it is your responsibility to forgive them. Unforgiveness is like a plague that just builds up over the years and eats away at you. Don't be the person who is consumed by bitterness and ends up living a life that's way less than what you deserve. Whatever your calling is in life, there is no pain that should pull you away from it. In fact I would argue (based on my own experience) that pain produces purpose. Remember that wherever you go and whatever you do in life. Know that above all things, God is with you, He will never leave you nor forsake you. And always act out of love. Thank you for reading, continue to walk faithfully.

55845478R00215

Made in the USA
Middletown, DE
19 July 2019